The prospect of entering the mall was suddenly terrifying.

And if she had to do something this demanding and dangerous, then most people would consider Neil Fletcher to be the best person she could have at her side. Kelly was quite confident that personal antagonism would have no impact on Fletch's integrity. She knew that if she needed guidance or protection they would be hers without request, as long as Fletch was capable of providing them.

The huge sliding glass doors of the mall entrance had been shattered. Kelly could feel the crunch of glass under her boots as she squared her shoulders and followed Fletch through the dark, gaping hole that had to be entered. Yes. She could trust Fletch as a partner in whatever horrors they might be about to face.

It was just such a shame that she knew the risk of trusting this man any further than that.

CITY SEARCH AND RESCUE

Life and love are on the line...

The Team
Dedicated professionals—
doctors, nurses, paramedics, police
and firefighters— trained to save lives
in urban disasters.

The Dangers
A crowded building collapses,
and in the aftermath of the disaster
the team must save innocent lives—
at the risk of their own...

The Romance
Passions run high as the dramas unfold—
and life and love are on the line!

CONSULTANT IN CRISIS
is the first book
of Alison Roberts's heart-pounding
CITY SEARCH AND RESCUE
mini-series.

The drama continues in Joe and Jessica's
story, followed by Ross and Wendy's
story—coming soon in Mills & Boon®
Medical Romance™!

Recent titles by the same author:

THE SURGEON'S CHILD
SURGEON ON CALL
EMERGENCY: CHRISTMAS

CONSULTANT IN CRISIS

BY
ALISON ROBERTS

MILLS & BOON®

To Paul
This one's for you so you won't need to steal it
off my bookshelf when you think I'm not looking.
With love

*First published in Great Britain 2003
Large Print edition 2004
Harlequin Mills & Boon Limited,
Eton House, 18-24 Paradise Road,
Richmond, Surrey TW9 1SR*

© Alison Roberts 2003

ISBN 0 263 18152 9

*Set in Times Roman 16½ on 18 pt.
17-0604-50933*

*Printed and bound in Great Britain
by Antony Rowe Ltd, Chippenham, Wiltshire*

CHAPTER ONE

'RESCUE team above. Can you hear me?'

The silence was broken by only the sound of a small piece of rubble, dislodged by a steel-capped boot, that bounced off a broken length of timber before hitting a half-buried sheet of corrugated iron. The next ten seconds were eerily quiet.

'Nothing heard.' Urban Search and Rescue team member Neil Fletcher looked to his right along the chain of people.

Kelly Drummond was finding a more secure foothold amidst the precarious surface of building debris. Her heavily gloved hand grasped a shaft of timber between the exposed nails as she leaned closer to the steep mountain of rubbish. Rubbish that had once been houses. Houses that had held, and might still contain, people. Using a rock held in her other hand Kelly tapped loudly on a protruding water pipe before using her voice.

'Rescue team above. Can you hear me?'

Kelly tilted her head until her safety helmet actually touched the rubble. She listened carefully. The sound created by tapping on a pipe would have carried much further than a human voice. Maybe someone trapped in the collapsed building and still alive could have heard the sound. Maybe she would hear them call out in return or hear tapping that might indicate their use of a similar means of communication. The seconds stretched out. Ten...eleven.... twelve....thirteen...

'Nothing heard.'

Joe Barrington was next in line. Solid, easygoing Joe was a paramedic, like Kelly. She had thought he would be the only person on this team she would know. After an involuntary glance to her left Kelly's wish that that had indeed been the case was beginning to feel familiar.

'Rescue team above.' The deep rumble of Joe's voice carried right along the ten people making up the human chain. 'Can you hear me?'

Kelly needed to push her safety goggles back into place but didn't want to move during the listening phase. Even a tiny movement could send debris tumbling and the sound might mask the whereabouts of a potential victim. A chill puff of wind sneaked inside the collar of the protective overalls and brought with it a mist of drizzle. Kelly closed her eyes for a few seconds. A month ago she had been sitting in the sun at a street-side café in Melbourne. Even three weeks ago she could never have envisioned herself in this situation. Part of an Urban Search and Rescue squad.

Working alongside Neil Fletcher.

She had recognised the possibility of seeing Fletch again. After all, she had chosen to come back to Christchurch and their careers weren't a million miles apart. But it had been nearly two years now. It was more than likely that an emergency department registrar would have headed overseas for post-graduate experience and then chosen a bigger centre to come back to if he had returned to New Zealand at all. Besides, it had been Kelly who had chosen to end the relationship and the decision had been the right one. The only one. She had come to terms with that a very long time ago and she had moved on. Sorted out what she wanted from life and made damned sure that she was going to achieve it. Even if she did cross paths with Fletch it would make no difference. No difference whatsoever.

'Nothing heard.' Joe sounded disappointed. He was probably as weary as everyone else on the team now. The search was physically demanding and, so far, unrewarding. They had located one victim, whose position had been marked with fluorescent orange paint on a small slab of concrete further down the hill. A large 'V' for 'victim' with an arrow pointed to the precise location. A line through the centre of the 'V' indicated that the victim was dead.

Information received on their arrival at the disaster scene suggested that at least two more people were missing—trapped somewhere inside this potentially lethal environment. Subsurface. Casualties that had not been buried had already been removed. An ambulance triage station was dealing with the wounded.

A temporary morgue held the less fortunate victims.

'OK, team.' The shout came from a man standing below the line. Their team leader, Ross Turnball, looked perfectly at ease with his environment. He balanced easily on the insecure footing and moved with a grace that advertised an enjoyment of physical challenges. 'Move forward one metre.'

'Avoid the overhang.' The order came from another man standing apart from the chain. The confidence that the safety officer, Kyle, displayed was less convincing. 'And there's a single piece of reinforcing rod above you, Kelly. I've marked it.'

Kelly could see the piece of twisted steel, its rust largely covered by the orange spray paint. She could also see the overhang of the concrete slab above her head to the left. The weight of rubble on top of the slab made it dangerous to get close to. Kelly didn't need reminding of the potential for aftershocks following the earthquake that had caused these buildings to collapse in the first place. Even a small tremor now could make precariously balanced debris a very real danger for the rescue team.

The careful spacing of the line of rescuers needed to be modified to accommodate the danger of the overhang. That meant that she and Fletch would have to increase the distance between them considerably. Kelly took a deep breath and began to move, remembering to kept three points of contact with the debris at all times. One foot, one hand, the other foot and then the final handhold. One more repetition should take her to her new position well to the right of the overhang. And Neil Fletcher would be well to the left. At least three metres away from her this time.

'Rescue team above. Can you hear me?'

Kelly could barely hear Jessica's voice at the far end of the line as the new series of calls began. With no hope of hearing any response from this distance it was all too easy to let her concentration lapse again.

How could she have been so confident that crossing paths with Fletch would make no difference? That first day of the USAR training course had dispelled that confidence big time.

The first thirty minutes had been almost unbearable. Having entered the classroom, Kelly had almost turned on her heel and walked out again. It had been so totally unexpected, seeing Fletch sitting there. The shock had taken her breath away, left her completely numb for a split second, and then a horrible sensation like pins and needles had travelled through her whole body. Her fingers and toes had still been tingling as she'd eased herself onto the nearest available chair. Talk about someone walking across your grave. Someone resembling King Kong had just landed on hers with steel-capped boots.

'Nothing heard.' The voice was much closer now. It must be Fletch's turn again. Unconsciously, Kelly braced herself for the sound of his voice.

'Rescue team above. Can you hear me?'

Kelly could hear echoes of his voice in the silence. Echoes sending fingers reaching into her past that could retrieve memories she'd thought she'd buried as effectively as this debris had buried its victims. Memories of passion. Of hopes and dreams that had seemed so achievable. Of a pain that hadn't been worth risking again. Did Fletch feel any of it? Kelly willed herself not to turn and stare at him. Of course he didn't. After the anger that her abrupt departure had, no doubt, generated he'd probably been relieved when she'd left. He'd never tried to contact her, had he? Never bothered to ask why she'd just posted back the engagement ring.

'I can hear something!' The excitement in Fletch's voice jarred Kelly into focusing. Had she been mistaken in thinking she could hear an echo of his voice? They shouldn't be working together. Not this closely.

A murmur ran down the chain of rescuers when Fletch raised his arm to confirm his suspicion. The sound was terminated by a sharp blast of a whistle.

'Silence on the site,' Ross shouted to reinforce the whistle command. 'Fletch—repeat your call.'

This time Kelly also raised her arm as she listened. Then she pointed in the direction from where she could hear the faint sound. To her left. Fletch was pointing to his right. The faint sound of someone groaning or maybe calling out was coming from just above the overhang. The line of rescuers was broken as Ross issued clear commands.

'Joe, go up two metres and then to your left one metre. Jessica, go up one metre and then to your right one metre. Owen, see if you can move to a position a couple of metres above and between Joe and Jessica. Kyle, double check for hazards.'

Team members moved to their new positions, fatigue replaced by a sense of anticipation.

'There's a void in here,' Jessica shouted. She moved a length of broken timber to reveal a triangle of clear space formed by a sheet of roofing iron resting on a ledge of rubble. 'I think I can see someone.' Her voice rose excitedly. 'Hello—can you hear me?'

Kelly couldn't hear the response clearly enough to make out the words but that didn't detract from the sense of satisfaction. They had located a survivor.

'Her name's Wendy,' Jessica relayed a minute later. 'She's breathing all right but can't move her legs. She thinks she may have been unconscious for a while.'

Kyle was spraying an orange 'V' onto the nearest available surface.

'Move a bit further to your left, Fletch,' Ross instructed. 'We don't know what position this woman is lying in. We'll need to start removing debris from a distance of three metres or so. Jessica, keep talking to her. Try and find out whether she knows of anyone else who may be trapped.' Ross looked away as he turned his attention back to the whole job. 'Fletch, Kelly and Joe, you can stay to shift rubble and provide any medical attention needed. We'll get a Stokes basket up to you shortly. The rest of you form a new line. We need to cover the rest of this sector. As far as we know, we still have one missing person to locate.'

Clearing rubble to gain access to the void was painstaking and slow. They couldn't risk collapsing the space the survivor was confined in and had to be careful not to make their own positions any less stable. The safety officer was supervising the operation and directing placement of larger pieces of shifted debris.

'Watch out, Kelly! You need two people to shift that plank.' Kyle shook his head. 'Fletch, give her a hand, will you?'

A long blast on the whistle, calling for silence, meant that Kelly did not have to acknowledge his assistance. Jessica paused in the reassurance she was delivering to their patient and they continued with their tasks as quietly as possible as the new line and hail search got under way a little distance above and to their left.

'Rescue team above. Can you hear me?'

New team members picked their way carefully up the disaster site, bringing with them a Stokes basket. The heavy-duty moulded plastic stretcher had handles and strap attachments along the top of its raised sides. A first-aid kit and other equipment was ferried up inside the basket.

It took twenty minutes to get close enough to actually start extricating the survivor. A change in the amount of light available to the team was an indication of both weather deterioration and approaching dusk but the teams worked on with steady determination. The line and hail search was now nearing the end of the last sector of this site. If no more victims were found they would probably have to deploy search dogs to try and locate anyone else confirmed to be missing.

'Wendy—we're really close now. It won't be much longer.' Fletch had taken over the reassurance of their patient. 'How are you feeling?'

'Not too bad. I'm going to be really glad to get out of here, though.'

'Can you move or feel your legs at all now?'

'I'm not sure.' The sound of coughing was magnified by the sheet of iron still covering Wendy. 'I don't think so.'

'Does anything hurt?'

'No.' Wendy coughed again. 'This plaster dust is the worst thing. It keeps falling on my face.'

The top of the corrugated-iron sheet had been cleared of debris. As they lifted it, their patient raised her arm to shield her eyes from the light. Fletch moved closer, catching hold of Wendy's wrist to feel for a radial pulse. Kelly knew he would be assessing her respiration at the same time and they all watched as he conducted a rapid survey to check for any obvious injuries or blood loss. 'Let's get a C-collar on,' he ordered. 'And line up the Stokes basket directly below us. We're going to need to keep spinal alignment when we move her.'

Kelly and Joe had attended many spinal injury patients in their careers in the ambulance service but it had never been this awkward to try and immobilise and extricate them. The stretcher had to be positioned to remain stable and every move the team members made had to be planned in advance and checked to keep themselves safe as well as ensuring that any injuries to their patient weren't exacerbated.

Once Wendy was securely strapped into the basket stretcher, the progress was still slow as the rescue team manoeuvred their burden down the slope. It took seven people to conduct the operation safely. Two people positioned themselves in front of the four people holding the stretcher basket. When all team members were secure enough to move their arms without losing their footing the stretcher was passed handhold to handhold until the two people at the back were free of the burden and now standing behind the stretcher. Then those two people moved carefully under the watchful gaze of the scout to position themselves ahead. Slowly, metre by metre, the stretcher was moved smoothly towards the base of the slope and the safety of waiting emergency service personnel.

As Kelly moved to a new position at the head of the stretcher for the fifth time she heard a shout from the team members still searching. Joe stared up the slope for a few seconds before nodding. 'Another survivor by the look of it.'

'Thank God for that,' Kelly murmured. 'I think we've all had enough of this for the moment.' She shoved her hand into the slot at the head of the stretcher. The gloves made the task a lot more awkward but at least they were providing some warmth as well as protection. Her legs were freezing.

Fletch was moving behind her. 'Why did you volunteer for USAR if you don't like it?'

'I didn't volunteer, actually.' Kelly watched Fletch reach level ground. Their task was almost complete. 'Somebody volunteered for me.'

Joe's eyes crinkled behind the plastic safety goggles as he grinned. 'That's true. She made the mistake of turning up in the boss's office on her first day at work. I was in there, having just discovered that my intended course partner had broken his leg and wouldn't be able to make it. Kelly had her arm twisted very thoroughly.'

'Your friend must have heard about the course.' Damp auburn curls were plastered against Jessica's cheeks. She looked cold and exhausted as she changed handholds. 'A broken leg seems like quite an attractive alternative right now.'

'You think you've had it tough! This mask was useless for keeping the dust out and I thought you guys were never going to find me.'

'You were in there for a long time.' Kelly gazed back at the mountain of debris as they lowered the stretcher to the level ground. 'Rather you than me, Wendy. Did you see any rats?'

'Rats!' Dark blue eyes widened dramatically behind the safety goggles. 'Nobody said anything about there being rats around here.'

Joe was unclipping the straps that held Wendy securely in the Stokes basket. 'It's a rubbish tip,' he reminded her. 'Rubbish tips are always full of rats.'

'OK, that does it.' Wendy sat up and lifted her goggles to sit on the brim of her helmet. She pulled the dust mask to hang below a small but determined chin. 'I resign. I'm not going to be a patient again. One of you lot can do it next time.'

'But you're so nice and light,' Kelly said. 'Imagine if we had to cart Joe down a hill. It would be a killer. He must weigh three times as much as you.'

'It's all muscle,' Joe protested.

'It's discrimination,' Wendy declared. 'And I'm going to take a stand. Short people shouldn't get picked on.' Her grin was disarming. 'Not while there's rats around, anyway.'

Ignoring the hand Fletch was extending to help her, Wendy steadied the stretcher by holding the sides, stood up quickly and then straightened to her full height of barely more than five feet. Fletch and Joe both towered over her and were grinning broadly. Wendy looked away, her eyes narrowing thoughtfully at the sight of the approaching figure.

'I know. Let's bury Kyle next time.'

'Mmm.' Jessica's quiet tone matched Wendy's. 'And let's not dig him up.'

It was unfortunate that the burst of laughter coincided with Kyle's small mishap. Picking his way down the hillside a little too eagerly, Kyle had slipped and travelled a short distance in an undignified sitting position. He looked less than pleased as he came to stand beside Kelly.

'What are you doing standing up, Wendy? You're supposed to have a spinal injury.'

'I'm miraculously cured,' Wendy announced.

Kyle looked around the group. 'You were supposed to deliver her to ambulance triage,' he informed them. He looked less than happy to find his authority undermined.

'There's nobody there,' Fletch said patiently. 'The exercise was location and retrieval, Kyle. We've completed that. Very successfully, in fact.' Fletch was smiling as he nodded. 'Well done, everyone.'

It annoyed Kelly that she automatically joined in the murmur of agreement and even appreciation. What was it about Neil Fletcher that made people unconsciously welcome and accept his leadership in almost any situation? Ross had been given the role of team leader for this training exercise and assessment but he was looking as happy as everyone else to have won Fletch's approval.

Kelly looked down the second Fletch's glance caught hers. She nudged the bright red plastic Stokes basket. 'I wonder if they want this taken back up the hill.'

'Doubt it. I think they'll be able to carry the last victim down by themselves.' Fletch sounded amused. 'It's only a tape recorder after all.'

Kelly hadn't noticed that the second half of the rescue team had already started its descent. One of their USAR instructors, Dave Stewart, was leading the group, and he had the strap of the case containing the tape recorder over his shoulder. Bursts of laughter punctuated the careful downward journey of the team and Kelly became as curious as everyone else to find out the cause of such amusement.

'Listen to this, guys.' Owen, one of the fire officers on the course, reached in front of Dave to push a button on the cassette deck.

The intermittent groans had been recorded by a woman who had clearly enjoyed her role of acting as an injured and trapped victim. The intensity and length of the groans varied and even Kelly had to giggle after a particularly enthusiastic rendition.

'Kelly!' Joe sounded shocked. 'Were you carrying a tape recorder on your last date?'

'And can I have his phone number?' Wendy had to raise her voice over the fresh burst of laughter from the group.

'I should be so lucky!' Kelly knew that the colour flooding her face would make her casual response less than convincing. She looked away, intending to find something she could focus on while she controlled her embarrassment. Instead, her gaze locked with that of Neil Fletcher. He appeared to be joining in the general mirth but the gaze from the dark hazel eyes was not even remotely amused. It was cold. Disapproving. Angry, even. Kelly gave up any hope of controlling the blush but her colour was no longer due to embarrassment. How could someone else's anger be so instantly contagious?

'Good to see that this has been so enjoyable.' Dave shut off the recording. 'We would normally have a debriefing of the training exercise here but I'm sure you're all cold and tired and it's getting dark. Let's pack up and get back to school. When we've all had a chance to get changed and clean, we'll get going. We're booked in for that meal at seven and we can do our debrief over a beer or two before we eat.'

'Excellent idea.' Owen and Joe led the move to collect gear. Cans of spray paint, the white-board that information about the incident had been recorded on, the Stokes basket, first-aid equipment and a large quantity of other gear was loaded into the luggage compartment of the bus. The large group worked well together, the impression that they were a closely knit team highlighted by their uniform of dark blue overalls, the bright orange safety helmets they wore and the frequent bursts of laughter that punctuated conversations. Everybody was happy to have completed a challenging day of practical work. Nobody was sorry to board the bus and leave the grim playground of the hard-fill rubbish tip behind.

The hot shower was blissful. Dressing warmly in her faded, comfortable jeans, a soft shirt and a fluffy llama wool pullover, Kelly bundled up the overalls which were now badly in need of washing and headed for the waiting linen bag in the female change rooms. The area was busy. Jessica was pulling a wide-toothed comb through her shoulder-length auburn curls and

Wendy was applying gel to spike her short blonde hair.

'I can't come out for this meal,' Jessica was telling Wendy. 'Mum needs a break from looking after Ricky. There's nowhere he can play outside at that motel we're in and he'll be bouncing off the walls by now.'

'Why don't you just come for the debrief and a drink and not stay for the meal? Or maybe you could ring your mum and get her to meet us there. Pizza restaurants are usually quite happy to have kids around.'

'Oh, I couldn't do that.'

'Why not?' Wendy spotted Kelly in the mirror. 'Hey, Kelly! Do you reckon we passed?'

'We'll find out soon enough, I guess.' Kelly was rummaging in her rucksack for a hairbrush. 'That's the only reason I'm going out for this meal.' Today's exercise had been more than putting theory into practice. It had also been an assessment of some of the skills they needed for qualification.

Jessica looked worried. 'I suppose I'll have to come.'

'Dave and Tony will understand if you can't,' Kelly told her. 'They know about Ricky.'

'Maybe I shouldn't have brought him with me.' Jessica put her comb away. 'But it seemed like such a great opportunity. He's never been near a city before and I couldn't have come if I hadn't brought him. Mum couldn't cope on her own for that long.'

'How old is Ricky?' Wendy was wielding a mascara wand.

'Nearly six.'

'He must be enjoying an extra holiday from school.'

'He doesn't go to school yet. He's...not ready for that.'

Kelly and Wendy exchanged a glance. The undertones were obvious but the close friendship that was developing between the three women had not yet extended to confidences about the problems Jessica's child clearly faced. Maybe a social occasion was a good idea for reasons other than finding out their test results.

'Is Ricky's father around?' Wendy's query seemed casual.

'No.' Jessica tried to match her tone. 'I'm single.'

'Me, too.' Kelly dragged the brush through long strands of her thick, dark hair. 'A permanent state, I suspect.'

'Don't be too sure. I thought it was for me, too.' Wendy peered thoughtfully into the mirror. 'You never know what—or who—might be waiting around the next corner in your life.'

'Too true.' The comment carried the weight of absolute sincerity. If Kelly had known that Fletch had been waiting, she would have been very careful to avoid this particular corner.

Jessica was smiling. 'You've only known Ross for two weeks, Wendy. You must be pretty keen on each other if you're so sure your single state is over.'

'When you meet the right person you just know.' Wendy's smile was confident.

'And does Ross feel the same way?' Kelly tried not to sound sceptical. She had felt that way about Fletch once. The euphoria of being in love made you believe all sorts of things that had no basis in reality. She almost shook her head. How could she feel so old and wise at the age of only twenty-eight?

'I think he did by the end of last weekend.' Wendy's confession was shy. 'We're going over to the Coast tomorrow. He wants to show me his house.' Her expression was now dreamy. 'He wants me to think about going to live with him and working at the Coast hospital.'

Kelly started braiding her hair into a single rope. She didn't want to hear any more about Wendy's dreams of a happy future. She didn't need the reminder of how her own dreams had been crushed. One way and another, this Urban Search and Rescue training course was proving to be a growth experience that was not entirely welcome. She pushed the thought aside and smiled as she made an attempt to change the subject.

'And if it doesn't work out with Ross, we all know who'll be only too keen to step into the breach.'

'Oh, please!' Wendy pushed her fingers through her hair to tousle the blonde spikes just a little more. 'Kyle Dickson gives me the creeps. Every time I look up he's staring at me.'

'He fancies you.' Jessica grinned.

Kelly had a momentary flashback to the stare she had received from Fletch during the teasing at the rubbish tip. Maybe unrequited passion would be a preferable emotion to deal with.

'Well, it's not mutual.' Wendy pulled on a polar fleece jacket. 'We'd better get going. They'll be waiting for us in the bus by now.' Her grin was impish. 'Hey, it's Friday night and we're two-thirds of the way through this course. It's definitely time to celebrate.'

Jessica checked her watch. 'It's nearly six,' she said despairingly. 'I *can't* come—even for a drink.'

'Then don't,' Kelly advised. 'Come on. I'll go with you while you explain things to Dave.'

Kelly was tempted to excuse herself from the outing at the same time but Wendy did have a point. It was Friday night. They had all worked hard throughout the week and it would be nice to relax. The class group of nearly twenty people was large enough to dilute the fact that she would be socialising in the same company as Neil Fletcher, and the likely alternative of spending another evening exercising her persuasive skills to deal with the situation at home found Kelly climbing into the bus quite happily.

The USAR course members made a sizeable group as they entered the popular pizza restaurant and bar housed in one of the more modern suburban shopping malls.

'Does anybody know what time the pharmacy here shuts?' Sandy was from a country town well north of Christchurch. Like several other people she was living in during the course at the school's accommodation facilities. 'I've run out of shampoo.'

'The supermarket will be open,' Wendy told her.

'Does anyone else need anything?'

'I'll come with you,' Kyle announced. 'I need a new razor.' At twenty-three, Kyle was the youngest member of the class. He stroked a chin that looked like it was struggling to produce anything more than fluff and then eyed

Fletch and Joe, who were collecting orders to take to the bar. 'Get a beer for me, will you, guys? We won't be long.'

Kelly chose a single seat at the end of the long table. With no other chairs available, Fletch would be forced to sit at the other end of the table and the conversation there was loud enough to easily drown out the sound of his voice. Things would be far more manage-able at this end as far as Kelly was concerned. Dave Stewart was already seated on her left and having an animated conversation with June, a lively woman in her mid-fifties who was probably the oldest of the class members.

'I was a cop, originally,' Dave was telling June as Kelly sat down. 'I'm forty-six now and I've spent the last nineteen years with the fire service.'

'How long have you been involved with USAR?'

On Kelly's right, Wendy was sitting beside Ross and they, too, were quickly engrossed in their own conversation.

'It's true.' Wendy was laughing. 'It was be-cause I was fat that I joined the tramping club at school. I wanted to lose weight. Next thing I knew I was hooked and running marathons!'

'Ever tried the Coast to Coast?'

'No, but I'd love to. A race across the south island in one day would be the ultimate. I'd need to brush up on my kayaking and cycling times, though.'

'I did it last year.'

'Oh, wow!'

Kelly was only half listening to the conversations around her as she kept an eye out for the return of Joe and Fletch. Her colleague and her ex-fiancé. It was kind of ironic that the two men had established such a good friendship over the space of the last two weeks but Kelly was confident that she had dismissed any curiosity on Joe's part on the first day of the course. During the class introductions, in fact. That session had probably been the hardest of the course so far. Kelly stole a glance at Dave as she remembered how he'd started that first day.

'You represent a wide group of expertise,' he'd told them. 'We have people here from the fire service and the Red Cross. We have paramedics, nurses and doctors. Some of you are from cities and some from rural areas.' Dave's smile had been welcoming. 'I suggest the first thing we do is go around the group and introduce ourselves.' He'd looked at Kelly. 'Tell us something about yourself. What you do and how you ended up being on this course.'

'Um...' Kelly had swallowed hard. She hadn't been at all sure she'd even wanted to be on the course any more. Three weeks of sitting in a room with Neil Fletcher? Being reminded of the overwhelming effects that being in love with him had had on both her mind and body? No, thanks.

The silence was loud. Everyone was listening, especially Fletch. Kelly wanted to escape, to run away. But she had never run from anything in her life and she wasn't about to start.

'I'm Kelly Drummond,' she stated clearly. 'I'm twenty-eight years old and I've been with the ambulance service for eight years now. I qualified as a paramedic while I was working in Australia and I just came back to a new job in Christchurch three weeks ago. I guess they decided it would be a good idea to throw me back in at the deep end and give me the challenge of learning about urban search and rescue.'

Joe introduced himself with his usual laid-back confidence. June offered her background of nearly thirty years with the Red Cross, and Owen, Roger and Gerry made it obvious that working together at an inner city fire station gave them a close bond. And then it was the introduction Kelly had been dreading.

'I'm Neil Fletcher.' The familiar deep tone was as disconcerting as the first sight of him had been. 'But, please, call me Fletch because I'm not likely to respond to being called Neil by anyone other than my mother.'

The laughter was general and the ice was broken amongst the group. Even Kelly smiled. She hadn't forgotten how he hated the name Neil.

Joe poked Kelly in the ribs with his elbow. 'Didn't you and Fletch get together for a while? Just before you took off across the ditch?'

'Not so you'd notice,' Kelly whispered back. 'I doubt that he even remembers me.'

Any suspicion that Kelly wasn't being truthful would have been allayed by the way Fletch had later brushed her off and pretended they were strangers. Kelly was relieved. It would make things a lot easier—at least for the duration of this training course. She was unsurprised. If she'd been in Fletch's position she wouldn't want her reputation tarnished either. Dr Fletcher would be more than slightly embarrassed if the sordid details of their break-up ever became public.

'Are you sure you only wanted an orange juice?' Joe leaned past Wendy to place a tall glass in front of Kelly.

'Thanks, Joe. That's perfect.'

Fletch was right behind Joe. 'Wine for you, June, and a nice cold beer for you, Wendy.'

'Oh, excellent! Thanks, Fletch.' Wendy looked around brightly. 'Drag a chair over from that table. There's plenty of room on either side of Kelly.'

'Of course, she only wanted orange juice.' Fletch nodded at Joe as he squeezed a chair in between Wendy and Kelly. 'Does she ever drink anything else?'

'How do you know that, Fletch?' Wendy was now completely distracted from her conversation with Ross.

Kelly cringed as she realised she wasn't the only person interested in the response to the question. She was grateful for Kyle's intrusion as he and Sandy joined the group again.

'So, what's the news?' Kyle demanded. 'I hope I haven't missed the debrief.'

'Couldn't start without you, Kyle.' Dave tapped on his glass with a spoon to call for silence. Kyle edged rapidly down the side of the table and slid into an empty seat next to Owen. Dave cleared his throat.

'OK, team. Let's get this debriefing over with. Our pizzas are going to turn up in a minute. You all did a great job today and I'm happy to say you've all passed your first practical assessment. Hazard markings, rubble crawl, line and hail search and patient extrication.'

A pleased murmur ran around the group. The three-week USAR course was punctuated by both written and practical assessments and each success took the participants closer to their goal of becoming qualified as members of a very specialised emergency service.

Dave caught Kelly's glance. 'Maybe you can get hold of Jessica later and let her know.'

'Sure.'

'Where is Jessica?' June queried. 'Not sick, I hope?'

'Family responsibilities,' Dave said vaguely.

'Oh…' June nodded understandingly. 'Her little boy is a special needs child, isn't he?'

'They're all special needs,' Joe muttered from Kelly's side. 'Kids get in the way of having any fun at all.'

Kelly wondered if Joe realised how evident his disappointment was, but maybe nobody else had noticed the spark of interest that Joe had extinguished the moment Jessica had mentioned having a child.

'You'll change your mind one of these days, mate.' Fletch leaned slightly across Kelly to speak to Joe. 'I can just see us all meeting for a ten-year class reunion. You'll probably have six kids by then.'

'No way.'

'Grandchildren are great,' June put in. 'I've just got my second one.' She chuckled. 'I'll probably be a great-grandmother in ten years' time.'

The relief Kelly had experienced when the conversation had been diverted from her drinking habits was replaced by an inexplicable sadness. Where would she be in ten years' time? Still focused on a career without any kind of real home or family? Her goals had been so clearly set but she had almost achieved them now. What could she aim for when she had succeeded in helping to sort out her mother's current situation and cut her own ties to an unhappy past at the same time?

'You got any children, Fletch?' Wendy's query came as Fletch turned his attention to his glass of beer with obvious relish.

'Not yet, but I'm working on it.'

Kelly was jolted from her own thoughts. She had wondered repeatedly over the last two weeks whether Fletch was in another relationship. The thought of it being meaningful enough to produce children in the foreseeable future gave her a distinctly unpleasant sensation.

'I intend to one of these days,' Fletch continued. 'Unlike Joe, I really enjoy the company of children.'

'I had four,' June told him. 'In fact, it was my daughter that got me involved with Red Cross in the first place.'

Kelly didn't want to listen to any plans Fletch had to start a family. Once again she was grateful for an interruption from Kyle, who called loudly from the other side of the group.

'Is that it, Dave?' He sounded disappointed. 'For the debrief?'

Dave nodded. 'We can pick over the details next week. I think we need some time out. And some food.' He waved at the waitresses carrying huge wooden platters in their direction. 'I hope you're coming our way.'

Kelly was hungry enough to enjoy the slice of Mexican pizza laden with hot peppers and sour cream. She had a slice of the vegetarian pizza that was offered next. The conversations around her were becoming increasingly difficult to hear as laughter from the other end of the table increased. Soon they were all listening to Gerry giving a convincing imitation of the kind of groaning they had heard the taped 'victim' uttering. Kyle was clearly more amused than anyone else as they rehashed their search for the groaning woman.

'I was sure we were going to find two people trapped under there.' Owen laughed.

'Would have been a sin to disturb them.' Roger chuckled and then winked at Kelly who smiled briefly before shifting her gaze.

Kyle took the opportunity to interrupt the last pocket of conversation left at the table. 'That's not the way we'd do it,' he informed the fireman beside him.

'You're a volunteer firefighter, Kyle.' The older man sounded tolerant. 'In a small, rural district. How much experience of big blazes do you get?'

'Enough,' Kyle responded defensively. 'We've had a serial arsonist at work for months now. The school got torched. And the church.'

'I read about that.' Roger looked interested. 'Have they caught the arsonist yet?'

'Probably kids,' Joe muttered.

'No.' Kyle clearly still wanted to prove his credentials. He ignored the distraction. 'Besides, I use the internet a lot. I've learned heaps about major fires. And USAR stuff.' Green eyes brightened as he grinned at the audience he'd collected. 'I've downloaded some great pictures of the Oklahoma bombing. I'll bring them in next week and show you.'

Roger had lost interest. He collected his empty beer glass and stood up. 'Can I get anybody another drink?' Spotting Kelly's empty glass, he moved down the length of the table. 'What are you having, Kelly?'

'I'm fine for now, thanks.'

But Roger was reaching for her glass. 'What was it? Vodka and orange?'

Fletch's raised eyebrow was uncalled for. His look of amusement was even more irritating.

'I don't want another drink, thanks, Roger.'

Fletch was still looking amused. 'Very wise, Kelly. You don't want to overindulge.'

Kelly forgot her intention to maintain the pretence they were strangers. She didn't like being patronised.

'You're certainly experienced enough in that department to be in a position to give advice.' Her tone was light-hearted enough to make Roger grin.

'So...you've got a reputation, have you, Dr Fletcher? How come Kelly knows and we don't?'

'There's nothing to know.' Fletch managed to sound convincingly surprised.

'Oh, come on.' Roger was still grinning. 'What was it, Kelly? A past filled with wine, women and wild parties?'

'Something like that,' Kelly agreed.

'How do you know?' Wendy looked curious. 'You weren't one of the women, were you?'

Joe was also looking at Kelly. His raised eyebrow expressed surprise that she'd got herself into this verbal corner. His shrug suggested that he couldn't think of any way to help extricate his colleague.

'I'm sure she was.' Roger's glance was appreciative. 'If Fletch had any taste, that is.'

'Taste was never one of my strongest points.' Fletch's grin made the comment a joke to everyone other than Kelly. 'Except for beer,' he added. 'I'll come with you if you're heading for the bar, Rog.' He stood up.

'Sure.' But Roger wasn't ready to move quite yet. He was still looking at Kelly, his curiosity unsatisfied. Fletch noticed the unspoken question as he waited. He shrugged offhandedly.

'Kelly and I knew each other,' he said casually. 'It was a long time ago. Before she went to Australia. And it was no big deal, was it, Kelly?'

'No.' Kelly's smile felt tight but she held Fletch's gaze as steadily as she could. 'It was no big deal.'

But it had been. Kelly had to force herself to break the eye contact with Fletch. It felt like a physical connection and it was suddenly unbearable. Their time together had certainly been a long time ago and maybe it hadn't been a big deal for Fletch, but it had been big for her. As big as it got. Kelly tried to shake off the dismay that threatened to overwhelm her as Fletch turned to walk away.

Maybe it still was.

CHAPTER TWO

SHE was late.

Neil found he was watching Kelly's hurried entrance to the classroom with as much attention as everyone else. There was a flush of colour on her cheeks that suggested annoyance. That figured. Kelly set high standards for herself and attracting attention by being late would not be acceptable behaviour. The long, dark ponytail swung across her back as she turned to push the door shut.

'Sorry I'm late.' Clearly embarrassed by disrupting a session that had already started, Kelly sat down beside Joe, flashing a rueful smile at her colleague before opening her rucksack to extract writing materials. Fletch wondered if the smile meant that Joe was privy to personal circumstances that had provided an unwelcome obstacle to her arriving on time. Unaccountably, the thought provoked a feeling of irritation.

'No problem, Kelly.' Dave wasn't feeling irritated. He was smiling at Kelly. 'Except that you're going to be running the first session this morning.'

'What?' Kelly's jaw dropped and Fletch suppressed the twinge of sympathy that replaced the irritation. Why should he care that her composure was now thoroughly ruffled? Why had she been running late, anyway? Had she slept in? Had someone been sharing her bed? Fletch settled back in his chair with an uncharacteristic frown. He wasn't going to help her out. No way.

Neither was her friend, Joe. 'We took a vote,' he told her cheerfully. 'And you're it.'

Kelly looked frankly worried now. Already dark blue eyes looked almost brown and a vertical crease appeared between them. Lord, had he forgotten what those glimpses of vulnerability had done to him? He had to fight the temptation to step in, to say something encouraging or comforting. She could cope. The Kelly Drummond Fletch had known had never backed away from a challenge. She didn't need anyone's support and she certainly wasn't about to get his.

'Cool.' The tiny head shake confirmed that Kelly was ready to handle whatever was about to be thrown in her direction. 'What is it? Hide and seek in the rubbish tip again?'

The groan was general. Some class members were still feeling the effects of that full-scale scenario.

Dave shook his head as he smiled. 'Today's session, as Kelly is about to find out, is medical. We're going to focus on developing basic skills in patient assessment, resuscitation and trauma management.'

Dave's attention shifted away from Kelly. It had only taken a few days for the class to divide itself into two distinct groups and Dave was directing his next words towards the less medically qualified course members who had come from the ranks of the fire service and civil defence.

'As USAR team members you may well be the first to reach an injured person. You may, in fact, be their only contact for some time. The team you are part of may not be fortunate enough to have the kind of medical expertise that we have represented here.'

Dave's glance returned to Fletch's side of the room. 'Today's course module will be redundant for some of you—Fletch and Ross as doctors, Joe and Kelly as paramedics and Wendy, Jessica and Sandy as nurses. It's not just because Tony and I feel like a day off that we're turning these sessions over to you guys. I expect we're going to learn something, too. We intend to take full advantage of your skills and knowledge.'

'Especially Kelly's.' Joe sounded smug.

'Your turn is coming, Joe.' Dave smiled at Kelly. 'Your name just came out of the hat first. I hope you'll all keep in mind that we're going for a strong emphasis on practical skills today. We're learning what we need to use in the field.'

'I'm hardly the most qualified person to start,' Kelly reminded Dave. 'You've got an emergency department consultant here, you know.'

The emphasis rankled. Was it so hard for her to use his name? To make him a person instead of a profession? Or had Kelly been surprised to discover that Fletch had gone from a registrar position to a consultancy in the space of only two years? Maybe thirty-two was young to have achieved such a senior position but it hadn't been easy. He'd worked extremely hard and he deserved his success. Everyone was looking at him now. Except Kelly.

'I disagree,' Fletch said calmly. 'By and large the trauma patients that turn up in Emergency have already been assessed and neatly packaged by the ambulance service. We work under controlled conditions with plenty of equipment and staff available. Hardly what we're going to encounter in a USAR call-out.'

Dave nodded his agreement. 'Don't worry, Kelly. You won't have to do it all by yourself. Your task is to take us through a primary survey. Ross is going to do vital signs and CPR. Joe's going to cover immobilisation techniques. Fletch is going to talk about shock and Wendy and Jessica are going to cover treatment of soft tissue injuries. This afternoon we'll try and pull it all together with some scenario work in small groups.' Dave gestured towards the space he had left at the front of the class. 'Over to you, Kelly. Let's get stuck in.'

Kelly looked quite relaxed as she moved to lean against the table at the front of the room, but that was because most people wouldn't know that the habit of tucking a tendril of dark hair behind her right ear only surfaced when she was nervous. Fletch knew. He also knew what she looked like when that magnificent mane of hair was unleashed from its restraint...when it fell like the softest curtain imaginable to screen a slim, naked back.

Shutting his eyes to kill the memories the sight of Kelly's hair evoked, and shutting his mind to the emotional effect that kicked in like a bad aftertaste, Fletch tried to concentrate on what the young paramedic was saying.

'A primary survey is a means of identifying life-threatening situations or injuries in order to treat them appropriately at the earliest opportunity.'

Fletch opened his eyes again. Now it was her voice that was stirring emotions he would rather not explore. It was a voice that had haunted him for months after she'd left. Deceptively soft, it belied a determination and courage that had been one of the qualities Fletch had admired most in this woman. He sighed inwardly. Last week he'd thought he'd had this unexpected reunion taped. He could handle seeing Kelly again. It made no difference. Had that brief confrontation at the pizza restaurant when they had made an acknowledgement, albeit understated, of a past relationship been enough to change things? Or was his resistance just wearing thin? Why was it that things that one knew to be self-destructive were still capable of exerting such a powerful attraction?

'Assuming that the scene has been made safe enough for us to approach our patient, what's the first thing we're going to do to start our primary survey?' Warming to her role as tutor, Kelly had written a series of letters on a whiteboard—S, L, A, B, C, D and E. S had just become the word safety.

Kyle, as usual, was the most eager to respond. 'See if they've got a pulse.'

'Are we going to check their breathing?' June was a grey-haired woman with many years' experience in civil defence work.

'Good,' Kelly responded. 'But what will we do as part of, or even before, that check?'

'Talk to them,' June expanded. 'Ask them if they're OK.'

Kelly ignored Kyle's dismissive head shake. 'That's exactly right, June. In other words, we're going to determine our patient's level of consciousness.'

Kyle slumped down in his chair and fiddled with his pen. Fletch watched as Kelly caught the attention of more people on the other side of the room.

'We won't worry about the more complicated methods of assessing LOC, like the Glasgow coma scale. Basically, we're going to find out if the patient is spontaneously responsive or whether he responds to vocal or painful stimuli.'

The group of men sitting near June were all listening carefully now. Owen was the oldest of the four fire officers from various city stations.

'What kind of painful stimuli are we going to use?'

'What about a pen?' Roger looked pleased to attract Kelly's notice. 'You put it between the fingers and then squeeze them together. Hurts a lot.'

Pens got picked up around the group and experimented with. Fletch was more interested in watching Roger. Why hadn't he noticed before that the younger fireman was rather good-looking? That he wasn't taking his own gaze off Kelly? Had Fletch missed something brewing between those two in the last couple of weeks? Roger had certainly been determined to find out what the past connection between Fletch and Kelly had been. If he was interested, then good luck to him, Fletch thought bitterly. He had no idea what he was letting himself in for.

'Try a knuckle rub on the sternum,' Kelly told the group. 'Just as painful and you don't need to go hunting for a pen. OK. Let's say there's no response. What next?'

'See if they're breathing?'

'Sure.' Kelly nodded at Kyle's suggestion. 'But there's something else we might need to do before that.'

Roger's gaze was still locked on their novice instructor. As though he felt the observation he was under from Fletch, Roger looked up. He stared back at Fletch for just long enough to issue an unspoken challenge.

'What could interfere with someone's ability to breathe?' Kelly prompted.

'Oedema,' Wendy responded. 'Soft tissue injury.'

'Being dead,' Fletch suggested dryly.

Joe snorted with laughter. 'Yep. That'll do it every time.'

Kelly's lips quirked. A tiny, one-sided curl and quick correction that Fletch recognised as easily as her hair-tucking gesture. A sign that his black humour had amused her but it was not appropriate to indulge the response. How often had Fletch deliberately evoked that quirk in the past? A private joke subtly hinted at in front of a patient, a not-so-subtle murmur in her ear as he passed. Did Roger have any idea how easily Kelly's sense of humour could be tickled? Fletch had always been able to make her laugh and he had taken enormous pleasure in doing so, especially when she'd been stressed or unhappy. Sometimes she'd appeared to be under perfect control but he'd known she'd still been laughing on the inside. A sparkle of glee had made those gorgeous blue eyes dance and Fletch had been able to hug the satisfaction that he had been the one to provide that enjoyment.

Not that there was any hint of sparkle this time. The look that Kelly threw both Fletch and Joe was purely exasperated. She walked towards the firemen. 'Owen, pretend you're a disaster victim.'

'No pretence needed,' Gerry quipped. 'He *is* a disaster.'

This time Kelly acknowledged the humour with a real smile. A quick grin that gave Fletch an odd sensation, as though he'd been kicked in the stomach by someone wearing very soft shoes.

'You've been trapped for a long time in a collapsed building,' Kelly continued. 'You're sitting against a wall. Your leg is caught under a timber beam. Oxygen level's getting low. You're in pain from a fractured femur and you've been bleeding from a laceration on your arm. Your blood pressure's dropping. Rescue isn't far away. You've been listening to them getting closer for hours now but you can't hold out any longer. You lose consciousness.'

Obligingly, Owen made a gagging sound and his chin dropped to his chest.

'Excellent!' Kelly's grin was broader this time. 'What's happening now?'

'He's snoring,' Roger observed.

'As usual,' added Gerry.

'He's obstructed his airway,' Jessica informed them.

'And if he's unconscious he won't be able to correct it.' Kelly nodded. 'It could lead to a respiratory arrest and death, despite imminent rescue and non-life-threatening injuries. So— we get into the space. There's no response. What do we do?' Kelly pointed at Owen's mouth. 'We'd do a rapid finger sweep just to check that his false teeth haven't fallen out and then...' She took Owen's chin with one hand

and his forehead with the other and as she tilted his head back to open the airway the snoring sound stopped. '*Now* we can assess his breathing.'

Safety, level of consciousness, airway, breathing and circulation were covered within twenty minutes. Assessing the level of disability and exposing the chest and abdomen to assess injuries took another fifteen minutes. Kelly was relaxed now and enjoying herself. She teamed the non-medical members of the class with partners who could coach them when she directed a practice of the skills she had covered. Amidst the lack of confidence some people had to overcome and the humour that lightened the more serious aspects of the subject was a willingness to learn and a new respect for someone who had been one of the quieter members of the class up till now.

'Kelly, my patient reckons he's bleeding to death from a ruptured artery. Do I fix that before the airway?'

'If he's telling you he's bleeding to death, his airway's fine. You can't talk if you're not breathing. You're onto circulation straight up in this case. Get some direct pressure onto the bleed.' Kelly looked up to address everyone in the room.

'Remember we're trying to identify the life-threatening problems in order to deal with them quickly. Don't move on to the next item on the agenda until you've managed whatever problem you find.'

'What if they stop breathing when you've finished the checklist?' Kyle was kneeling beside June with his hand gripping her wrist.

'Then go back to the beginning and start again. There are three things that are going to kill people very quickly—respiratory arrest, cardiac arrest and severe haemorrhage. We have to identify and try to rectify those situations.'

Dave called a halt to the session. 'That was fantastic, Kelly. Thanks.'

The spontaneous applause from her students made Kelly blush but she looked happy. Somehow, that irritated Fletch. Or was it that Roger's appreciation was so noticeable that was the annoying factor?

'We've spent over an hour learning some very important skills but don't forget what Kelly said. A primary survey should only take thirty to sixty seconds.' Dave paused for a moment as a few people made some last-minute notes. 'Ross is going to run us through what vital signs are and how to measure and record them. Then we'll have a break for morning tea.'

The break was welcome. Fletch had not enjoyed the morning so far. He felt out of sorts. The unwelcome memories Kelly had stirred surely weren't entirely responsible for his mood. He had learned to deal with those memories long ago and he couldn't care less if the attraction that Roger the fireman was advertising was reciprocated. The irritation was augmented by a faint touch of nausea that Fletch knew he couldn't blame on the odd beer or two he'd had with a mate the night before. He knew what the cause was likely to be and he headed for the men's toilet with a decisive stride as soon as Dave signalled the timetable break.

The small pouch fitted into the back pocket of his jeans as neatly as a wallet. Fletch unzipped the pouch and removed the contents. He was so focused on his task that it wasn't until the door swung open behind him that Fletch realised his mistake.

'Damn!' The drop of blood fell from the end of his finger and splattered the side of the ceramic handbasin.

'*Fletch!*' Ross Turnball sounded shocked. 'What *are* you doing, mate?' He stepped closer. 'Oh... I had no idea.'

Fletch had a new drop of blood on his finger now. He touched the end of the test strip to the drop and watched the blood travel up the central line. The beep signified that the device had started its measurement. The result was only thirty seconds away. Fletch rinsed his finger, still cursing inwardly that he'd forgotten to shut himself into the privacy of a cubicle.

'It's not something I advertise,' he told Ross curtly.

'Are you insulin dependent?'

'No.' Fletch smiled wryly. 'Quite the opposite.'

Ross raised an eyebrow. 'That sounds un-usual.'

Fletch pulled the test strip from the device and threw it away. 'Four point one,' he mur-mured. 'I just need a bit of morning tea.' He glanced at Ross as he packed away his kit. 'It's a long story,' he said casually. 'Remind me to bore you with it some time.'

Low blood sugar was not the culprit as far as Fletch's mood was concerned. Maybe it *was* being close to Kelly that was disturbing his equilibrium after all. With a cup of coffee in one hand and two biscuits in the other, Fletch moved away from the class group. He found a seat around the side of the building that had the advantage of being in full sunshine, but the pleasant solitary respite didn't last long.

'OK, I'm dead curious.' Ross sat down be-side Fletch. 'You can tell me it's none of my business but my professional instincts are mak-ing me nosy. How long have you been a dia-betic?'

'Two years.'

'And you get hypoglycaemic even though you don't take insulin?'

'Not too often these days, fortunately,' Fletch responded. 'I still need to keep a close eye on my levels, though, especially if I'm not well or under stress or miss a meal or something.' He bit into a biscuit. 'I just don't usually make it public.'

Ross nodded. He sipped his own coffee before breaking a thoughtful silence. 'How were you diagnosed?'

'Hypoglycaemic crisis,' Fletch said quietly. 'Rather a dramatic one, apparently. A taxi driver left me in the middle of the road. Someone called an ambulance and said I was so drunk I was a danger to myself. I was having a grand mal seizure by the time I got delivered to the emergency department and went into a coma after that.'

'Good grief! Sounds like a major crisis.' Ross stared at his companion. 'Did you have some kind of insulin-secreting tumour?'

Fletch looked impressed. 'You're more clued up that my doctors were. I was in the intensive care unit for three days before they came up with a definitive diagnosis.'

Ross was nodding. 'An insulin-secreting islet cell carcinoma. Not malignant, I guess, or you wouldn't be looking like you do now two years down the track.'

'No. I'd be dead,' Fletch agreed. He grinned. 'Never a good look.' His smile faded. 'Waiting to find out whether it was malignant or not wasn't much of a joke.'

'I'll bet it wasn't.'

'It was a rough ride all round, actually. I had a partial pancreatectomy. When I got through the complications of pancreatitis and amazed the specialists by surviving, it was decided that my prognosis wasn't so bad after all. I was in hospital for ten weeks altogether and I came out looking like I'd spent time in a concentration camp. It was another three months before I was back at work.'

Ross shook his head. 'Amazing story, Fletch.'

'Not one that I want spread around, mate. I don't let it interfere with my life but some people would be inclined to regard it as an obstacle to a reliable performance.'

Ross nodded briefly. 'Nobody will hear anything from me.' He gave Fletch a curious glance. 'This wouldn't have anything to do with the hint of an atmosphere I detected between you and Kelly the other night, would it?'

'You could say that.' Fletch's tone was grim. 'We were an item...briefly. When she found out how sick I was she decided she didn't want to deal with it. She left a message with my flatmate to say she wasn't hanging around. I came out of my coma to find I'd been dumped.'

Ross whistled silently. 'Hard to believe anyone could be that callous.'

Fletch's snort was derisive. 'One way to test a relationship, I guess. I reckon she did me a favour in the long run.'

'I'll bet it didn't feel like it at the time.'

'It was a fair kick in the pants,' Fletch agreed lightly. 'Along with the glimpse of my own mortality, it made me sort out my priorities. I concentrated on getting fit and then took a good look at my career. I'd been cruising for too long. Having fun and not taking anything too seriously. That had a big shake-up.'

'No more wine, women and wild parties, then?'

'Wasn't difficult.' The lopsided smile was a little poignant. 'Kelly cured me of trusting women and I got too involved in post-grad studies to have time for any parties—not that they were that wild, anyway. I got my consultancy last year and I have big plans for where the emergency department is heading. Disaster management strategy and this USAR stuff is just my latest hobby.' Fletch stood up. 'Speaking of which, we'd better head back inside, mate, before we start any rumours.'

The subject matter had made it an easy day for Kelly. If only she didn't have the background worry about what was happening at home right now, it would have been a very enjoyable day. There had been no answer to her phone call at lunchtime. How long could it take to visit someone and tell them face to face that there was no going back? That decisions had been made and would not be changed. Face-to-face meetings were dangerous, Kelly knew that. But maybe her mother was right in saying that such a confrontation was essential for closure. Maybe it was the fact that she hadn't been brave enough to do it herself that had left this uncomfortable impression that there was unfinished business between herself and Neil Fletcher.

Not that Fletch seemed bothered. If it had been an easy day for Kelly, it must have been downright boring for the emergency medicine specialist. The session he had taken on shock had been excellent. Unfortunately, Kelly had been distracted from using the tutor's expertise to advance her own knowledge. The excuse to observe Fletch for such a long period of time had been irresistible and it was the first time she had allowed her gaze to remain on the man for more than a second or two.

Two years had left their mark. Fletch looked thinner. The brown hair was worn a little shorter these days and were those highlights still sun-streaked blond or had some grey crept into those soft waves? Kelly's fingers actually tingled as the memory surfaced of just how soft those waves were.

'So. We've defined shock as a state of widespread inadequate perfusion at a cellular level. What are the things we need for adequate perfusion?'

Kelly glanced away as Fletch looked in her direction. She wasn't about to contribute any suggestions. She was too busy trying to figure out what the difference in Fletch's appearance was. It wasn't anything physical making him seem so unfamiliar. It was something to do with his manner. He was scribbling on a whiteboard now. Perfusion relied on a functioning pump, an intact set of plumbing and an appropriate volume and content of fluid. Fletch was making the physiology lecture very user friendly for non-medical people. Even funny at times.

That was it. That was the difference. Fletch's humour and his smile had a different quality. It was more restrained and less frequent. Fletch had never been a serious type. The way he had made Kelly laugh had been why she had fallen in love with him in the first place. Virtually the moment they'd first met. Kelly could remember that first meeting as though it had happened yesterday. Fletch had been a new registrar in Emergency and Kelly had come in with a patient at the end of a long, hard day. The patient had been drunk—found comatose under a hedge with two empty rum bottles nearby. His level of consciousness had improved enough for him to become abusive on the way into hospital and Kelly had had enough. Finishing a long day with her least favourite type of case had been enough to noticeably test her professional manner.

'This man presented with a GCS of eight, hypotension and bradycardia,' Kelly informed the triage nurse. 'There is evidence of an ETOH overdose.'

Fletch heard the tail end of Kelly's handover as he walked past. He glanced at the empty rum bottles now lying on the end of the stretcher. He leaned towards the triage nurse and spoke in a stage whisper.

'The technical medical term is "totally pissed".'

Kelly controlled her threatened giggle more effectively than the triage nurse.

'We don't have any details on the patient other than his surname.' Kelly took another glance at Fletch who seemed in no hurry to move away. 'Which appears to be Ikkey.' She spelt it out.

Fletch looked thoughtful. 'Icky,' he repeated. He eyed the evidence of recent vomiting on the stretcher blanket and then winked at Kelly. 'He is, rather, isn't he? That's another technical term I went to med school to learn,' he added to the nurse beside them.

'Cubicle three.' The triage nurse was grinning broadly now. 'Fletch, he's all yours. In fact, we'll make sure you get every icky patient that comes in from now on.'

'I don't know,' Fletch grumbled. 'Here I am sharing my professional knowledge and what thanks do I get for it?'

The humour rescued Kelly's day and it was so easy to accept that first invitation for a date with the new registrar. That humour underpinned the whole relationship, in fact. Fletch could make anything funny and yet his jokes often displayed a real sensitivity. They helped to achieve a closeness that Kelly had never had with anyone before. Or since. She loved that sense of humour more than anything about Fletch. Not that he couldn't be serious when he needed to be. He could turn it off in an instant and look intense and serious. Like he did when dealing with an emergency. Or, in a very different way, when he was about to make love to her.

Oh, help! Kelly had to shut her eyes to stifle that particular jog down memory lane. There was no point going there. Things had changed. Fletch had changed. Maybe he'd grown up finally and the change had made him more trustworthy. No. Kelly clamped that train of thought down as well. Her father had taught her only too well how little credence could be placed on any promises or even intentions of becoming trustworthy when it came to that kind of behaviour. And it wouldn't make any difference now, anyway. Not with the opinion Fletch now held of her.

Joe's session on immobilisation techniques had been a lot more fun. The quips about bondage and the good-natured teasing of Wendy and Ross now that their relationship was public had made the time pass swiftly. Wendy, Jessica and Sandy had made a good job of soft tissue injury management and the practical scenario at the end of the day would have been a great way to finish if only their instructors hadn't put her and Fletch into the same group, where she'd also had Kyle to contend with. Wendy had been coerced into being a patient again. This time she had been a crush injury victim with a slab of concrete on her leg. Cardboard boxes had represented the hazards they had marked and the surrounding debris had been removed, allowing access to their victim.

'Hi, there, Wendy.' Fletch shifted a last piece of 'rubble'. 'Here we are, finally.'

'Check her airway,' Kyle said excitedly. He reached out and Wendy ducked her head instinctively to avoid the physical contact.

Kelly suppressed a sigh. 'We've been talking to her through the wall, Kyle. She's been answering us. She's told us she doesn't have any breathing problems. There's no sound of respiratory distress and her respirations are normal depth and rate. We can probably assume her airway is patent.'

Tony was supervising their scenario. 'Airway *is* patent,' he told them, 'but the respiration rate is 30 and shallow. What are you going to do next, Kelly?'

'Check circulation.'

Kyle reached for Wendy's wrist. 'Good radial pulse,' he said happily.

'No.' Tony shook his head. 'Pulse is weak and thready. Tachycardia of 120.'

'I'll do a body sweep.' Kelly smiled at Wendy's look of relief as she got in before Kyle to run her hands down each side of their 'patient's' body.

'No evidence of major haemorrhage,' Tony confirmed.

'We're assessing the general condition as we look at our patient,' Fletch contributed. 'Her colour is good and she's not diaphoretic.'

Tony smiled. 'Your patient is pale, sweaty and cool to touch.'

'We want to check for neck tenderness and put a C-collar on if it's indicated.'

'No neck pain,' Tony decided.

'She's in shock,' Kelly said. 'We need to get an IV line in and start some fluids.'

Wendy gave a convincing groan. 'My leg *hurts*,' she moaned.

'We need some pain relief on board as well,' Fletch murmured.

Kyle shook his head impatiently. 'Her leg hurts because she's got a dirty big bit of concrete on top of it,' he stated. 'What we need to do first is get rid of it.' He made a show of putting real effort into shifting the polystyrene 'concrete' slab. 'Now we can extricate her,' he announced with satisfaction. 'Let's go, team.'

'No hurry now, Kyle,' Fletch said dryly. 'You've probably just killed our patient.'

Kyle's grin faded as it dawned on him that Fletch was being serious.

'That was a large piece of concrete, Kyle. Fortunately it would have taken more than one person to shift it, which would have given us time to give some prophylactic treatment for a crush injury.'

'But it was the concrete causing the injury. The sooner it gets shifted the better. It's hardly likely to kill her.'

'Actually, it could,' Kelly told Kyle. 'We were told in the scenario set-up that Wendy had been trapped like this for more than twenty-four hours. Crushed tissue exudes toxins and when you move the weight the toxins get released into the body. The patient can die very suddenly and very quickly due to a cardiac arrhythmia.'

Kyle's face tightened angrily and his voice rose. 'How the hell am I supposed to know something like that?'

'You're not,' Tony said quietly. 'The lesson here is that no unilateral decisions should be made. Especially by the least medically experienced person on the team.'

Other groups in the classroom had finished their scenario work. Kyle's angry query had attracted attention and people edged closer to see what was going on with the crush injury scenario.

'How would you have dealt with this, Kelly?' Tony queried.

'I've only dealt with one serious crush injury victim before and we worked under a radio link to an emergency department at a major hospital in Melbourne.' Kelly searched her memory eagerly. 'We gave a huge fluid loading of four or five litres of saline. We didn't have some of the drugs indicated so we had to make do with what we had. We gave Ventolin and glucose and insulin and I think it was atropine.' Kelly frowned. 'It's a while ago now.' She looked directly at Fletch without hesitating. 'How would *you* deal with it?'

'That sounded like a pretty good pre-hospital regime. Kelly's quite right,' he told the group that had now gathered and were listening with interest. 'Treatment has to start before the weight is removed. Hypovolaemia has to be treated aggressively and the hyperkalaemia treated prophylactically.'

'Hyper— what?' Kyle was trying not to look totally disgruntled.

'High levels of potassium,' Fletch explained. 'It gets released by damaged cells and it causes fast, irregular heart rhythms that can lead to an arrest.'

'What's the rationale for giving glucose *and* insulin?' Kelly asked.

'To counteract hyperkalaemia. It's the insulin that does that. Was it a short-acting form you used?'

'I think so.'

'Giving glucose will encourage the body to produce more insulin further down the track.'

'And the atropine would have been to counter a tachyarrhythmia?'

Fletch nodded. 'Sodium bicarbonate would have been useful as well. And calcium.'

'They were the things we didn't have.'

'Did he survive? Your crush injury victim?'

Kelly smiled as she nodded. 'He lost the lower part of his leg but he lived to tell the tale. He'd been trapped under his car for three days out in the bush. It was a helicopter rescue job.'

'You were on the helicopters?'

Kelly opened her mouth to respond but Tony cut in to call their attention back to their scenario. 'Let's save the stories for later,' he suggested. 'Everybody else has finished and I don't know about you guys but I'm starving.'

Not being able to tell Fletch about the drama-packed events of helicopter rescues was disappointing. Kelly also wanted to know about the chemical interaction between insulin and potassium. For the space of that interchange Kelly had forgotten the past. She had only been aware of how encouraging Fletch's admiration could be and how stimulating gaining knowledge from him was. The disappointment became more intense as they packed up for the day. Fletch wouldn't want to talk to her again. Not like that. Not unless she could find a way for other people to initiate a discussion.

Kelly Drummond had been the only woman who had ever given Fletch exactly what he needed on so many levels. They had shared the same, frequent amusement in often totally inconsequential aspects of life. They had shared a passion for careers that had overlapped enough to allow communication that hadn't needed background explanations. The mutual physical passion was something Fletch was determined not to remember. And he could have done without the reminder of the intellectual stimulation that conversation with Kelly could spark.

It would be so easy to talk to her again. Really talk. Their discussion on crush injury syndrome had, briefly, taken him back to a time and place when such an interchange had been a highlight of his day. His interest had been caught to the point when he hadn't wanted to stop talking. He knew just how eager Kelly was to learn more about the subject and he knew that she would absorb and remember every piece of information she could glean. He hadn't wanted to stop listening either. He wanted to know about the dangers Kelly had faced working on a helicopter rescue team, wanted to hear stories of lives saved and the type of emergency medical practices currently being used in such a front-line field.

Dangerous territory. And Fletch was not going to be lured anywhere near it. There were only a few more days left of them being cooped up in close proximity on this course and it should be easy enough to avoid any contact that could run away into personal communication.

That avoidance was, in fact, even easier than he had anticipated. The next day was taken up with theoretical work and practical demonstrations of shoring techniques and methods of assessing structural safety in partially collapsed buildings. Then there was a day for the protocols of co-ordinated incident management systems and practice using different kinds of radio equipment and data collection. More detailed work on identifying and dealing with hazards followed that and suddenly they were all revising flat out for the final written exam. The course was over and the final paper would give Dave and Tony the chance to collate marks. If they passed they would be issued their personal protection kits on Friday afternoon. They would have their basic equipment and would be available to respond to call-outs from then on.

It was a long wait after they finished the exam. The questions they had answered were discussed endlessly over a late lunch.

'The signal to evacuate the scene—it's three short blasts on a whistle, isn't it?'

'Yeah. And one long blast and one short one to resume operations.'

'I got confused about the timber shoring. Rakers and sole plate cleats.' Jessica sounded worried. 'I'm sure I've failed.'

'That's nice-to-know information. I doubt that it's essential,' Fletch reassured her. 'A major scene will have engineers to deal with the technical side.'

'And you can always call the fire department,' Owen added. 'We've got the equipment and muscle to deal with most of that kind of stuff.'

'A cubic metre of concrete weighs 2.5 tonnes. And steel is 8.2 tonnes.' Kyle was checking his notes. '*Yes!* I got that one right.'

'I just want to get the results,' Kelly sighed. 'It's been a long three weeks.'

'Hasn't it just?' Fletch's quiet agreement didn't appear to be directed at Kelly but she could feel the implications. He hadn't enjoyed being thrown back into her company. Maybe he had found it just as disturbing as she had.

Finally the wait was over. They assembled in the classroom. Boxes of gear lay in front of their instructors. Overalls and helmets, head-lamps, goggles and dust masks. Elbow and knee pads, gloves and whistles.

'The ID cards are temporary. You'll be issued with formal IDs once your results are processed by the national qualifications authority.'

The class was silent.

'Wendy? Congratulations, you've passed. Come and get your card. When we've finished you'll be able to sort out your kit.'

Wendy flushed with pleasure at both the result and the applause. She sat down, clutching her card.

'Fletch? Congratulations.' Dave shook his hand. 'It's been a pleasure having you as part of the group.'

June, Owen, Roger, Joe and Sandy collected their cards. Jessica's worries had been unfounded. Even Kyle had passed the course. Kelly felt confident that her turn was coming. Surely they wouldn't announce a failure in so public a manner?

The pager Dave wore on his belt sounded as Kyle sat down. A moment later, Tony's pager sounded. The instructors exchanged a surprised glance.

'I'll ring them,' Tony said. 'You carry on.'

Gerry's turn was next. Then June's friend, Pamela. Then Bryan, another fireman. Tony came back and spoke quietly to Dave, who listened intently. They kept talking. Now Dave was looking around the class and nodding. What was going on? The class members exchanged glances. The atmosphere held an unmistakeable air of anticipation. Dave cleared his throat.

'This couldn't have been timed better,' he told them. 'We have a code blue activation under way. There's been a major building collapse in town. There's an unknown number of victims trapped and all available USAR personnel are being called in.' Dave paused for just a second. 'That now includes all of you. I want you to come and collect your kits and any personal gear you might need, like medications and toiletries. We'll meet at the bus in fifteen minutes. Let's go.'

Nobody moved. Kyle smiled knowingly as he broke the stunned silence. 'It's another dummy run, isn't it? It's not for real.'

'It's as real as it gets, Kyle. Let's move.'

Dave sounded serious and everybody stood up, albeit reluctantly.

'Funny time for another practice,' Owen was heard to mutter. 'I thought we were all going to the pub to celebrate.'

'Maybe that's where they're taking us,' Joe suggested. 'Let's play along so we don't ruin the surprise.'

'Kelly!' Dave was calling over the increasing level of noise in the room. 'Sorry—almost forgot. Here's your card. Congratulations,' he added as Kelly reached the front of the room. 'Make sure you collect all your gear. You're going to need it.'

'Sure.' Kelly was quite prepared to enter into the scenario. It was a novel way to end a course. She pulled on her overalls and checked that the helmet she had chosen was a good fit. Jessica was pulling goggles from a box beside her.

'This had better not take too long,' she told Kelly. 'I've arranged to meet Mum and Ricky at a toy shop in town. Ricky's going to choose a new toy car as a present for being so well behaved this week.'

'We'll probably just go around the block,' Kelly said. 'I don't think they'll be going to too much trouble to make this realistic.'

Kelly had to revise her opinion as the bus passed a third intersection without indicating any turn that might take them back to the classroom's location or a nearby tavern. She wasn't the only person to notice the police car that shot past them a short time later at high speed with its lights and siren blazing. At the next intersection she could see the build-up of slow-moving traffic, but it was a Friday afternoon. Traffic in town always got heavier when schools finished for the week.

Traffic didn't usually come to a complete standstill, however. Or get blocked by a barricade of police vehicles. And there was never the sound of so many sirens approaching from different directions. And Kelly had never seen a pall of smoke that hung over the suburban mall she knew lay at the end of the main road they were on. The same mall they had visited only a week ago.

'Oh, my God,' she said aloud.

Heads turned and necks craned to see what Kelly had spotted from her window.

'What is it, Kelly?' Wendy called from the far side at the back of the bus.

The silence was expectant. Kelly swallowed hard.

'This isn't a dummy run,' she told them. Her voice trembled slightly. 'I think Dave was telling the truth. This is as real as it gets.'

CHAPTER THREE

THE unimaginable had to be faced.

Awareness of the enormity of what lay ahead came in stages. After the initial shock accompanying the realisation that the incident was genuine, a stunned silence permeated the bus. Its passengers stared silently through the windows, absorbing whatever information they could gather. The queue of traffic slowed to a crawl as they were allowed to pass the police cordon, still several blocks away from the mall. The sensation of unreality was as marked as the silence. Only a week ago this same group of people had travelled in this bus towards the same destination. Then they had been anticipating a convivial social occasion at a popular restaurant and bar. The anticipation now was so different it was incomparable.

Through the front windscreen of the bus Kelly could see the convoy of army vehicles ahead of them. The open backs of the trucks revealed large numbers of personnel, dressed in army fatigues. They looked young and keen to reach their destination. It was probably the first time they had faced involvement with anything more than a dummy exercise and Kelly could remember that kind of excitement. When she first joined the ambulance service any priority call would start the adrenaline flowing. Who knew what she would have to deal with at the end of the run? The sound of the siren advertising the importance and urgency of the mission only added to the expectation.

They could hear sirens now. The bus had to pull over and halt as an ambulance edged past. Kelly watched as Kyle stood up on the other side of the aisle, craning to follow the emergency vehicle's progress through the traffic. His stare was intense and remained unbroken despite the jerk that forced him to sit hurriedly as the bus resumed its forward motion. The smile on his face was probably unconscious. Kyle was as caught up in the excitement as any of the young army personnel. Fletch was also watching Kyle from his position in the seat in front of Kelly. He turned his head.

'He's got a lot to learn, hasn't he?'

'Mmm.'

They knew. Kelly and Fletch had faced countless emergencies and dealt with human tragedies they would never forget. They had both faced challenges that could provide enormous satisfaction when successful and sometimes devastating emotional repercussions when they weren't. They knew. And Kyle Dickson had absolutely no idea. It gave Fletch and Kelly a bond that was unavoidable. Kelly found herself smiling gently as she responded to Fletch's comment. The bond was welcome. What she was about to face was bigger than anything she had faced before and she was only too aware of how hard it might prove to be. It was comforting to know that someone else understood.

The smile tugged at something deep within Fletch. It spoke of a bond that needed no words to reinforce the understanding between them. More than that even. It indicated a bond that linked them in a way that couldn't be broken. A connection that Fletch had never even found a hint of with anyone else and one that would be there for the rest of his life even if he never saw Kelly again. And that was precisely the core of the pain their separation had caused and it was still able to stir a grief that even anger couldn't obliterate. His fleeting response to Kelly's smile was unconscious and was more a surprised reaction that such a deeply personal emotional reaction could occur in circumstances such as they were in right now.

The smile was so brief it almost hadn't happened. It was easy enough to dismiss the imagined sadness in the expression as Kelly chose the same moment as Fletch to turn away. He was probably just feeling the same sense she was of the daunting enormity of all this. Kelly looked through the rear window of the bus. They were being followed by a huge truck loaded with supplies of timber. Behind that was a four-wheel-drive vehicle emblazoned with the logo of a major television channel. An ambulance passed them, going in the opposite direction, travelling carefully with its beacons flashing. The lights in the cabin were on and Kelly could see someone adjusting the flow of IV fluids.

'I wonder how they're coping at Headquarters?' Joe leaned towards Kelly from two rows down the aisle. 'I imagine it's chaos.'

'I'd like to know what Emergency is like,' Fletch responded. He frowned. 'I should be there. We've just set up new strategies for dealing with major incidents. It's my job to co-ordinate them.'

A tow truck went past. Another one could be seen unhooking a car to join a line of vehicles blocking a side street.

'They must be emptying the mall car park,' Joe observed, 'to make room for emergency services.'

So where were all the people who had been unable to drive their cars away? Were they injured or dead? Or were they trapped and waiting for rescue? How many people were missing? And how soon would the passengers in this bus be allowed close enough to the scene to start trying to help? Questions tumbled around the vehicle. Speculation provided conversation but the answers were unavailable despite Dave's and Tony's constant telephone communication with whoever their commanding officers were. As they entered the vast car park still being emptied of private vehicles, Dave stood up.

'Stay on the bus once we've stopped,' he instructed.

Police officers wearing bright reflective jackets were directing them to an area near where the army trucks were parking.

'Tony and I will report to scene command and find out what's happening,' Dave continued. 'We'll get back and brief you all as soon as possible. I suggest you check your gear and make sure you have all your personal protection equipment ready to go.'

Kelly could see the fire engines flanking the main entrance to the mall with ladders extended to the second storey. Someone was being carried down. She could see the huge ambulance triage tent that had been erected. Scene command vehicles from the police, fire service, ambulance and civil defence were grouped together and there were people moving everywhere. It looked totally chaotic at first glance but closer attention revealed the purposeful direction of human traffic. The fire crews were focused on an area just out of sight round the corner from the main entrance. Hoses and equipment were being handled and moved with professional efficiency. An ambulance was being loaded with two stretchers outside the triage tent. A second ambulance was backing in slowly ready to take its place.

Fletch was clearly frustrated at having to stay where he was. 'They've got ED doctors working in the tent,' Kelly heard him inform Ross. 'That's where we should be right now. Doing something useful.'

'We may be more useful inside,' Ross responded. 'We've got skills now that they don't have.'

'It'll just be the surface casualties they're treating right now,' Joe added. 'People that were able to walk out or be accessed easily.'

'And if there's this many, it's highly likely that a lot of people are still inside,' Kelly said quietly.

'It doesn't look that bad,' Jessica commented.

'It's a huge mall. The main damage is probably further in,' Kyle said confidently. 'It must be bad. Look at all the extra equipment they're bringing in.'

Trucks carrying generators and lighting systems were being unloaded. Another vast tent was being erected and they could all see the huge crane that was slowly approaching the scene. They made themselves as ready as they could. Kelly tied on her knee pads and checked the lacing of her boots. She pulled the band from her ponytail and began braiding her hair tightly to keep it more securely out of the way. Jessica followed her example and tried to pull her auburn curls back to confine them with a scrunchy.

'Dave and Tony have been gone for half an hour.'

'I saw them with a group of people near the main entrance.' Wendy had been at the front of the bus for a while. 'I think they all went inside for a look.'

'I want to go inside,' Kyle complained. 'How much longer are we going to have to wait?'

Fletch had been watching Kelly as her fingers twisted the sections of her hair. He turned towards Kyle and sounded irritated.

'As long as it takes,' he said.

'It'll be too soon for Pamela, however long it takes,' Wendy told them. 'She's sitting in the front seat, crying. She says she's not ready for this.'

Jessica bit her lip. 'I'm a bit scared, too,' she admitted. 'I never expected this.'

'None of us did,' Fletch said. 'But we're here now and we're needed and we're all capable of doing whatever they ask of us. We're part of a team here. Nobody's going to be on their own and there's going to be people other than us in charge. We just need to follow instructions and do the best we can.'

Everybody was listening, including Kelly. Leadership came so naturally to Fletch and he was so capable of encouraging people to do their best—even do better than they thought they were capable of. Kelly had seen him do

it time and time again. She had always admired
the calm way he had been able to take control
of serious cases in Emergency. To pull a team
together and keep them focused on whatever
challenges they'd faced. Kelly hadn't been the
only person to have complete trust in his
judgement or to respond to his words of praise.
No wonder he was a consultant already.

'I still can't quite believe this.' Jessica
shook her head. 'If this had happened last
week, it could have been you guys trapped in
there.'

'I'd like to know what caused the explosion,' Joe murmured.

'I was going to come here today,' Jessica
mused. 'There's the best toy shop in town here
and I promised I'd bring Ricky before we went
home. And I wanted to try the pizza I missed
out on last week.'

'This is taking so long,' Kyle muttered.
'When are we going to get told something?'

'Don't be in too much of a hurry, Kyle.'

'Yeah. Save your energy,' Joe added. 'I
have a feeling that we're going to be here a
hell of lot longer.'

Jessica caught Kelly's eye. 'Can I borrow your mobile phone, please? I'd better call the motel and let Mum know I'll be late.'

'If people *are* buried, we might be here for days,' Roger observed. 'Who knows?'

'I can't stay that long,' Jessica said firmly. 'I might not even be able to stay all night. I'll have to see how my mother's coping.' She held the phone to her ear.

'They'll be calling in other USAR-trained personnel,' Fletch told Jessica. 'I'm sure they'll be able to replace you before too long. I guess we were just the easiest group to activate quickly.'

'And the most recently trained.' Sandy looked nervous. 'I hope I can remember everything we've learned.'

'Other people will be more experienced,' Kelly said.

'How?' Fletch raised an eyebrow. 'When was the last incident like this that they could have gained experience from?'

'There's never been anything like this. Oh, look...' Wendy pointed out of the window. 'That TV crew is arguing with the police.

They're obviously not too happy about being told to go away.'

'And here comes Dave.' Fletch was looking past the altercation.

Jessica closed the phone and handed it back to Kelly. 'There's no answer from our motel unit,' she said anxiously. 'I'll have to try again later.'

'There's going to be a formal briefing in the tent that's just gone up beside the triage area,' Dave announced as he stepped up into the bus. 'It should start in ten minutes. Extra USAR team members are arriving and we'll split you up into teams as soon as we have a better idea of numbers. You can expect to get specific instructions and to start operations as soon as the formal briefing is over.'

'What do you know so far?' Fletch queried.

'This is big,' Dave said soberly. 'Huge. A massive explosion occurred at about 3.30 p.m. in the central mall. It's brought part of at least three shops down into the supermarket area.'

Kelly checked her watch. That had been nearly three hours ago. 'How many people are involved?'

'At last count there were seventy-six people reported missing but there are calls from all over town to the helpline. Anyone who can't find someone is ringing to suggest they might have gone shopping. The mall *was* crowded. There could be a lot of children still in there.'

'Oh, God.' The sentiment was collective. Nobody wanted to think about having to rescue children.

'Let's get moving.' Dave cut off the buzz of reaction. 'You'll hear everything I know at the briefing.'

Kelly's group mingled with dozens of other people in the tent. Various uniforms indicated the origins of some teams such as the army and police. New people wearing USAR overalls joined the class, taking their numbers well above twenty. They greeted Dave and Tony and talked to everyone nearby, finding out what they could in advance. It took some minutes for silence to finally fall as the group on a makeshift platform called for everybody's attention.

'My name is Terence Drake.' A microphone was not necessary. Kelly was not the only person listening intently and the silence was complete. 'I'm the scene commander here at present. It's my job to give you the most up-to-date information we have and an overall picture of the size of this incident. You will report to your individual team leaders for operational instructions.'

An overhead projector was being used to display an image onto the canvas walls behind the podium. A map of the mall and surrounding streets was shown. The red dot of the laser pointer Terence Drake held circled the central area of the map.

'At 1538 hours this afternoon a large explosion occurred within the EatFresh Supermarket. This caused a structural collapse affecting a wide area, including these shops on the second storey.' The red dot paused on a fashion store, a hair salon and then a café. 'As far as we can tell, what remains of these stores is now in the supermarket area.

'The areas immediately surrounding the worst affected area are deemed structurally unsafe and are, as yet, unable to be accessed. This affects a further ten stores, although some appear outwardly undamaged.'

The dot moved to a new area of the map. 'The basement car parking area is also deemed unsafe and cannot be entered at this point. Engineering experts and support teams are currently assessing the damage and starting the process of making these areas safe for rescue personnel to access.'

Terence put down the laser pointer. 'Major evacuation procedures were put into effect immediately. The mall was crowded due to it being just after school hours on a Friday. Emergency services were on the scene within five minutes. The fire on the south side of the mall has been contained and the utilities of power, water and gas have been isolated.'

Dave Stewart was nodding. He had already received this information.

'Walking casualties have now either been evacuated or made their own way from the main area of the mall. However, we know there are uninjured people trapped in one of the lifts and in upstairs areas unable to gain access to a stairwell or fire escape. The fire service has just gained access to the second storey on the north side of the mall and they have started evacuation.'

Another figure moved forward. 'So far we have one hundred and four casualties, twelve seriously injured victims and three fatalities. People reported missing at present total around sixty but this figure is dropping as hospital admission lists are published. We have a lot of parents still panicking about the whereabouts of their children.'

Jessica caught Kelly's eye. Her expression conveyed empathy for those parents.

'Barriers to the operational area are being strictly enforced.' The scene commander took over speaking again. 'You are all reminded to follow the instructions of your team leaders and remain within the delegated areas for your assigned tasks. Ensure that protocols for safety are upheld at all times. One of my priorities is to avoid adding to the number of victims this disaster has already claimed.'

Kelly followed her team back towards the bus when the briefing was over. Another bus was parked beside theirs now and a canvas awning covered the space between the vehicles. People Kelly didn't recognise were arranging desks and portable lights within the covered space. A large whiteboard was propped against the side of one bus.

'You'll be working in four-to six-hour shifts,' Dave informed them. 'Accommodation is being set up in a church hall just out of the main car park on Sutherland Street. The mall has been divided into six sectors and we'll have enough personnel to put a team into each sector. The team will consist of a squad leader, five rescuers and one or two medics. Team lists will be put on the board shortly and each team will be briefed separately by their operations officer.'

Dave was looking at Fletch. 'I'd like to introduce Dr Neil Fletcher to those of you who haven't met him. Fletch is an emergency department consultant. I've arranged for him to liaise with hospital and ambulance service managers to put together the kits the medics will carry. We'll have a briefing for medics after the teams have been sorted. Fletch, take

Kelly with you and report to the scene command unit. That's the big grey truck close to the triage tent. They're expecting you and should have some supplies ready. We'll catch you up with anything you need to know after you get back.'

Kelly had to trot to match Fletch's long stride. He slowed fractionally.

'What supplies should we carry, do you think?' He seemed to be thinking aloud. 'We can't manage more than a bum bag or a small backpack.'

'OP airways,' Kelly suggested. 'IV supplies. Saline. Morphine.'

'We'll need metaclopromide and Narcan as well, then, to handle any side effects.'

'Splints.' Kelly could see a woman being helped into an ambulance. One side of her face and a shoulder were red and blistered. 'Burn dressings,' she added.

'The first-aid supplies can go in the Stokes baskets,' Fletch said. 'I'm talking about what we carry while we're searching.'

'Stethoscope and BP cuff,' Kelly suggested. 'We won't know how much we'll need until we can assess them properly.'

'We need to minimise gear to deal with life-threatening situations. We don't need to carry a sphygmomanometer to estimate blood pressure.'

'All right, then. We'll need intubation gear and an ambu-bag.' Kelly wondered how many more of her suggestions would fail to find approval.

'I suppose you'd like to carry a defibrillator around with you as well?'

'I don't know why you're bothering to ask my opinion,' Kelly snapped. 'Why don't you just decide what you want and get on with it.'

'That kind of autocratic behaviour might be your way of dealing with things, Kelly. It's not mine.'

'What's that supposed to mean?' Kelly could see the scene command unit they were heading for.

'I'm talking about your ability to make a decision and follow through without having the decency to even communicate with the people it's going to affect. Hardly the attitude for a team player, is it?'

'We'd better hope we're not on the same team, then, hadn't we?' Kelly pressed her lips together. Right now was not an appropriate time to delve into personal history. 'I don't think you'll find your attitude shared by others.'

'That's probably because they don't know you as well as I do. What do you think Dave or Ross or Joe would say if they knew you were capable of dumping someone just because they got sick?'

'*Sick!*' Kelly gave Fletch an amazed stare. Then she snorted. 'I suppose that's *one* word for it.'

'What word would you choose?'

'Diagnostic,' Kelly snapped. 'Or revealing, maybe. There are a few things people don't know about you, too, Neil Fletcher.'

Fletch paused abruptly and Kelly almost bumped into him. 'I would prefer to keep it that way, thanks.'

'I'm sure you would,' Kelly said angrily. 'And you can keep your opinions of me to yourself. You've got no right to complain about any lack of communication. It's not as if you bothered at the time, is it? You didn't try and find me. You didn't even have the decency to apologise.' Kelly knew they should not be having this conversation. Why on earth had Fletch picked this particular moment to start dragging skeletons out of the closet?

'*Apologise!* You've got to be joking.' Fletch was staring at Kelly with total disbelief. 'Apologise for what, precisely?'

'As if you didn't know.' Kelly shook her head. 'Oh, come *on*, Fletch.'

'Are you Neil Fletcher?' The voice cut through the arctic stare they were both locked into. 'We're waiting for you. The ambulance service has just unloaded supplies for the USAR medics to carry.'

Fletch turned away, dismissing the interaction with Kelly. Heaven knew why he'd risen to the bait like that. Maybe the tension of the situation was responsible. He had known it would be a pointless exercise. The nerve of the woman. *He* had been the injured party as far as their relationship was concerned. If anybody needed to apologise, it certainly wasn't him. Kelly was right. They'd better hope they weren't working on the same team.

The team lists were on the whiteboard by the time Fletch and Kelly returned to the USAR base. They would be deployed as and where needed within the six designated sectors of the incident area. Two of the teams were made up of mostly qualified people who had previously trained and practised together. The majority of the newly qualified class had been split amongst the remaining four teams. The squad leader for USAR 3 was Tony Calder. June was included amongst the rescuers and the medics were Joe and Jessica. Ross and Wendy were the medics for USAR 4 and Kyle was one of the rescuers on that team. USAR 5 was being led by Dave Stewart. Fire officers Owen and Roger were rescuers and the medics were listed as Fletch...and Kelly.

They'd have to organise a swap, Kelly decided. She could work with Joe or Ross, and Jessica or Wendy could be in Fletch's team. She would have a word with Dave as soon as the medics' briefing was over. As Kelly packed the supplies into her bum bag she glanced up frequently, trying to locate her squad leader, but when she eventually approached Dave he was busy issuing gear and instructions.

'Check your headlamps. There's no light at all inside yet. USAR 3, you're going to sector 6 with Tony in about ten minutes. Check your radio frequencies and test them. USAR 5, we're going in now. Sector 3 has been cleared by the engineers as safe to search. Roger, do up your helmet strap. Kelly, get your heavy gloves on. Are you all ready?'

The series of nods was the signal Dave was waiting for. He led his small team towards the barriers blocking the mall entrance.

There was no way to swap teams now. Kelly walked between Owen and Fletch. If she was really honest with herself, Kelly didn't want to be on another team, anyway. The prospect of entering the mall was suddenly terrifying. And if she had to do something this demanding and dangerous, most people would consider Neil Fletcher to be the best person she could have at her side. She had no trouble dismissing the errant doubt as to whether Fletch could be trusted to use his considerable skills with the utmost professionalism. Kelly was quite confident that personal antagonism would have no impact on Fletch's integrity. She knew that if she needed guidance or protection they would be hers without request as long as Fletch was capable of providing them.

The huge sliding glass doors of the mall entrance had been shattered. Kelly could feel the crunch of glass under her boots as she squared her shoulders and followed Fletch through the dark, gaping hole that had to be entered. Yes. She could trust Fletch as a partner in whatever horrors they might be about to face.

It was just such a shame that she knew the risk of trusting this man any further than that.

CHAPTER FOUR

NO TRAINING course could have prepared them for this.

The half-demolished house and even the mountain of rubble at the hardfill tip had been toys by comparison. This was real and the initial impression of relative normality only served to give the journey the quality of stepping further into a nightmare.

They had eaten at this pizza restaurant only a week ago. Through the shattered glass frontage Kelly could see overturned chairs in the dim interior, abandoned meals on the tables, a leather jacket, a woman's handbag and a child's toy lying beside a deserted pushchair. The fear had been enough to force people into a panicked escape that had left no time to gather precious personal possessions. The toy was a tired-looking stuffed rabbit. Would the child be missing it by now? Unable to sleep because of the loss? Kelly could imagine the noise of the explosion, the mother scooping up her child and fleeing in terror…the screams of distraught and injured people.

The lights from eight headlamps cast beams that moved as the team turned their heads, absorbing information from their surroundings. They became spotlights, picking out small pieces that were building into a jigsaw scene of overwhelming magnitude. A gift kiosk in the middle of the wide, tiled walkway had been overturned. Had the explosion been forceful enough to do that or had the structure been in the way of too many people trying to escape? Artificial flowers lay scattered amongst shards of broken pottery. A puddle of blood had been stepped in repeatedly, leaving skid marks and footprints that showed up in stark contrast to the pale tiled flooring.

It took a minute or two for Kelly to make sense of the sounds she was hearing. Visual impressions became more muted as she concentrated on the voices around her.

'Remember to stay alert at all times for indications of secondary collapse,' Dave was reminding them. 'Watch for columns and walls

out of plumb, sagging ceilings or water seep-
age. Feel any vibration or movement and listen
for creaking or rumbling noises.'

There were noises everywhere. Sounds of
heavy machinery and cutting equipment being
moved or used at a distance. The crackle and
buzz of the radio communication gear as people kept in touch with their teams. The USAR
team was not alone inside the mall. The partially damaged areas on the outskirts had been
searched already and were now being reassessed. Army personnel were clearing some of
the debris from the walkways to facilitate entry
and to provide a clearer escape route should it
be needed. The gift kiosk was being disman-
tled and removed.

The scream that cut through the closer
sounds made Kelly flinch. They all stopped
walking.

'What the hell was *that*?' Fletch's face was
in shadow behind the beam of his headlamp
but Kelly could see the lines of focused concern. A prickle of perspiration broke out down
the length of her spine. The sound had been

inhuman in its intensity but its echoes carried the undercurrent of suffering.

The sound came again. Drawn out this time. Long enough for analysis of its origin. Mechanical, thank God, not human.

'It must be the lift shaft,' Owen decided.

'They were going to try and raise it from the roof,' Dave nodded. 'It was stuck between floors.'

They should be nearing the end of the first wing of the shopping centre soon. Kelly knew it joined a central atrium that led to department stores and the supermarket.

'Don't forget there's another level below us,' Dave warned his team. 'Be aware of how stable the surface you're walking on is and watch out for altered elevation.'

Kelly nodded. She remembered the example of the Oklahoma bombing incident that Tony had used during a lecture on hazards. A fire-fighter had fallen four floors from basement level 2 to basement level 6 after stepping through a doorway. Then there was the only death amongst rescuers from that disaster, where a nurse was killed after being hit by a computer falling from above. 'Look Up and Live' was the catch phrase drilled in by their instructor.

They had a level above them now. Kelly looked up and stopped walking again. Jagged beams poked into a darkening sky ahead of them. What should have been the ceiling over the atrium had been partially obliterated. The end of the mall had not been apparent because there was no space for it to join. It was a pile of rubble reminiscent of the hardfill tip but far more daunting and dangerous.

This was real.

There were no tape recorders hidden amongst this wreckage. No co-operative class members safely tucked into a well-shored void, waiting to be discovered. There were real people trapped in here.

And some of them could still be alive.

Kelly took a deep breath through the filter of her dust mask. Her own fear was forgotten. They had a job to do and it could mean the difference between life and death for someone. Maybe for many people. She looked around at her team members to find Fletch was watching her. He smiled gently as though he had read her thoughts and knew she was ready. Then he nodded agreement. Fletch was also ready.

Where would they start? They couldn't climb over this wreckage and call to try and locate survivors. This was no neat hill of compacted debris. Walls and ceilings had toppled but Kelly had no idea what pattern of collapse was involved. Was it a curtain-fall collapse? A lean-over or lean-to floor? Or was it a tent or cantilever collapse that would mean accessing voids and confined spaces? It looked like a medley of all the patterns they had studied and it was nothing like the textbook diagrams. Kelly waited, along with the rest of the team, for instructions from their squad leader, but Dave was having a conversation by radio link to the scene commander. He moved about as he spoke, staring back in the direction they had come from, and seemed to be identifying their location.

'We passed the pizza place on the left as we came in. Then there were two or three clothing stores and a shoe shop. We have a jeweller's on the same side and a children's clothes shop opposite. We're blocked at this point by a major structural collapse.'

Dave moved ahead of the team by a few strides. He tested and then climbed onto a sloping concrete slab, ducking his head to clear a huge steel beam. His headlamp was sweeping in a large arc, the focus of which was concealed from those still at ground level. He was nodding.

'Yes. I think so. I can see a gap and what looks like the back of the bookstore.'

Kelly didn't hear the message Dave was receiving as noisy pneumatic equipment was activated nearby. She could, however, sense that action was imminent. Dave was climbing back down towards them.

'Roger, got that.' Their squad leader sounded decisive. 'We'll do our best.' He lowered his radio. 'There's a group of people trapped in the back of a pharmacy,' he told the team. 'They've managed to make cellphone contact. The shop backs onto the west mall which is at ninety degrees to the section we're in now. Our team is closest so we're going to try and locate them. There's a bookstore beside the pharmacy and it looks as though we can access that from here.'

'How many people are in there?' Fletch was right behind Dave as he led the way forward.

'Ten. Three are badly injured by the sound of it.'

It wasn't as terrifying as Kelly thought it would be. She had to concentrate so hard on where she was placing her hands and feet, trying to assess stability and to listen and watch for hazards, that there was no space left for personal fear. The pile of books she stepped on was slippery, however, and the momentary loss of control gave her a nasty jolt. She was grateful for the hand that caught her arm and steadied her. She gave Fletch a nod of thanks.

Part of the bookstore was relatively intact but it was impossible to tell if the shelves were against the wall bordering what remained of the pharmacy.

'Space yourselves along this wall,' Dave instructed. 'We'll see if we can hear anything.'

The long blast on his whistle called for silence. The signal was repeated and followed by shouts that echoed down the lengths of the intact portions of the mall. By the time the team had positioned themselves it was as quiet as it was likely to get. The pneumatic cutting gear being used somewhere overhead was the last to stop. Kelly was first in line. She used the metal stapler she had found to bang on the shelf space she had cleared of paperback books.

'Rescue team here,' she yelled. 'Can you hear me?'

The waiting was nothing like the practice scenarios. Kelly wanted desperately to hear something. The seconds ticked by. They were all waiting and listening.

'Nothing heard,' Kelly said.

It was Owen's turn then. And then another rescuer. Then it was Fletch.

'Rescue team here.' His voice seemed so loud. Surely it would carry through more than one wall. 'Can you hear me?'

Kelly could hear nothing. The tension mounted. They had to be close.

'I can hear tapping,' someone called.

Kelly could hear it now, too. She could feel it when she put her hand against the wall.

'I can hear a voice.' Dave pointed to his right. 'Let's shift the line and start again.'

This time they could all hear the response.

'We're in here... We need help!'

'We'll get to you as soon as we can.' Owen was at the point where the voice was loudest. 'We're just organising some equipment to get through the wall here.'

Dave was on the radio, relaying information and organising back-up. They needed gear to cut through and support the hole they would have to make in the wall. They needed help to move people and first-aid supplies to treat the injured. Progress seemed to be so slow to Kelly. Available space restricted the number of rescuers that could get close. Manoeuvring bulky equipment was difficult and time-consuming.

Fletch had taken up the position where voice contact was clearest. He had introduced himself to the pharmacist and was directing him to assess the injured as best he could. Kelly could hear the faint shouting from beyond the barrier of the wall.

'It's a head injury. It was bleeding badly but we've almost stopped that with pressure. He says he's got a bad headache and feels sick.'

'See if he can tell you what day it is and where he is. Are you able to check his pupils and see if they're equal sizes?'

'It's pitch black in here,' the pharmacist responded. 'We're in the dispensary and there's no windows. The lights went out when the explosion happened. Do you know what caused it?'

'No. Nobody does yet.'

'Was it a bomb?'

Kelly blinked. The idea that this disaster could have been deliberately caused hadn't even occurred to her. That sort of thing didn't happen here in New Zealand, even if the terrorist threat was international these days. Bali had been close but, then, that was a popular tourist resort. Why would they pick an ordinary suburban shopping mall in a city like Christchurch? No. There had to be another explanation. A mains gas leak, probably.

'How's the young woman?' Fletch asked.

'Lisa? She's unconscious again. She's still breathing but I can't feel a pulse on her wrist any more.'

'And the man with the chest pain?'

'He's a bit better. I gave him some of the GTN spray he'd come in to collect and he's had some aspirin.'

'You're doing a great job,' Fletch told him. 'How's everybody else?'

'Scared. How long before you can get us out?'

'We're nearly ready to start cutting this wall. Can you move people back as far as you can?'

Kelly also had to move away to let the fire service start work. She went as far back as the entrance to the bookshop. A Stokes basket was there, laden with supplies. She crouched beside it, checking its contents and keeping out of the way of an increasing number of rescue workers. The gap they had crawled through from the first mall had been expanded. Timber shoring was being used to strengthen the sides and loose debris was being shifted to leave a clearer accessway. Kelly had no idea of the time but it all seemed to be taking far too long. She hated being kept from treating an emergency. The longest she had ever had to wait had been over an hour once, when it had been a major operation to cut victims clear of a car wreck, but the extrication had been full on and she had been able to get close enough to touch her patient. She had been able to start oxygen and an IV. The pace was so slow now. Every move had to be considered and deemed safe before continuing.

'Here we go.' People near Kelly moved forward as a woman was led out of the bookstore. She was stumbling. Her skirt was ripped and her face and hair almost white with a covering of thick dust. Her tears were leaving tracks through the layer of dirt. A blanket was quickly draped around her shoulders.

'Come with me.' Someone was supporting the woman. 'We'll get you out of here.'

An older woman was carried out next. 'She's not injured,' Kelly was told. 'Just exhausted and frightened.'

Two teenaged girls came next. One was silent and staring blankly ahead of her as she was guided through the debris. The other girl was sobbing hysterically. Kelly wanted to get back to the front line of the operation. Was Fletch on the other side of the wall yet? Able to assess the injured? She had to wait as another dust-covered man carrying a child was helped over the rough ground surface.

'Let one of us carry your daughter, sir. It might be safer.'

'No. I'll carry her myself. Just show us the way to get the hell out of here.'

Kelly could move in now. Owen helped her with the Stokes basket. Fletch was crouched on the floor as Kelly crawled through the breach that had been created in the wall.

'The sooner we get you out to the ambulance area the better.' Fletch was nodding at the man in front of him. 'That broken wrist can wait for splinting. I'm more concerned about this chest pain you've got.'

'I can still walk. It's just my angina.'

'I think it might be a bit more than that this time.'

'I'll be fine. I just want to get out of here. The rest of this place could come down any minute.'

'We wouldn't be in here if that was the case.'

Kelly edged past Fletch, hoping he was right. In any case, the fear would not be helping this potential cardiac patient's condition. Fletch turned to an older man who appeared uninjured.

'You need to get out now, too, Bob, and get yourself checked.'

'I'm fine. I can stay here and help you. There's two more people hurt in here and they're a lot worse.'

'I've got the help I need now.' Fletch flashed Kelly a grim smile as she eased past. 'Bob's the pharmacist who's been doing such a great job in here,' he told her. Kelly nodded. She was focused on the two patients nearby, one of whom was lying motionless.

'Airway's clear and breathing's OK,' Fletch said. 'And the man who's sitting beside Lisa there is conscious. We need to collar both of them before we move them.'

Kelly nodded again. The pharmacist and the man with chest pain needed to be taken out to give them room to get the more seriously injured people out. She bent over the unconscious woman to reassess her airway and breathing.

'Lisa,' she called. 'Can you hear me? Can you open your eyes?'

The woman's eyes fluttered and then closed again. Kelly leaned closer. At least there was some response and she could be heard.

'I'm Kelly,' she told her patient. 'I'm a paramedic with the rescue service. We're going to get you out now.'

The woman mumbled words that were unintelligible. Bob turned back from the hole in the wall that Fletch was guiding him through.

'She's frantic about her kids,' he said. His voice caught. 'She's got two little girls. They were both in a pushchair. Lisa was buried. I dug her out but I...I couldn't find the children.' Bob was sobbing now and Kelly could see that the skin on his hands and arms was shredded. The pharmacist had clearly been desperate to locate Lisa's daughters.

'We'll look for them, Bob,' Fletch said. 'We have the experts here now. And the equipment. You've done all you could—and you saved Lisa.'

Kelly listened to Lisa's chest with a stethoscope. She pulled the remains of the woman's clothing aside to look for chest and abdominal injuries. Lisa was in shock, her blood pressure dangerously low—probably hypovolaemia due to internal bleeding. Kelly hadn't been able to find any evidence of major external haemorrhage from her body sweep. The breathing was rapid and shallow but clear. There were no serious chest injuries interfering with respiration. Kelly looked up a moment later.

'Lisa has a fractured pelvis,' she informed Fletch. 'There's no radial pulse and the brachial's barely palpable. I'm going to start an IV.'

'Great.' Fletch had brought a cervical collar back from the Stokes basket after seeing the last two patients evacuated. He was fitting it to the man who was sitting with his back against a pile of debris. Incongruous bright sparkles from hair clips and headbands shone in the beam of her headlamp amongst hot water bottles, hairbrushes and shampoo bottles.

Kelly unzipped her pouch and tied a tourniquet around Lisa's upper arm. She selected a wide-bore, 14-gauge cannula. This woman urgently needed fluids to bring her blood volume up. With a pelvic fracture she could be bleeding out internally and Kelly could only hope they weren't too late. How long since this injury had occurred? It had been more than three hours since the explosion before the USAR teams had entered the mall, and how long had they been inside now? Kelly had lost all track of time.

Two IV lines were up and running by the time Fletch had packaged the patient he was working on. A still bleeding head injury had been dressed, a cervical collar put on to protect the patient's neck and the Stokes basket had been used to move him due to the lowered level of consciousness and potential spinal injury. Kelly had a portable oxygen cylinder with her now. Lisa's eyes opened again as the high-concentration mask was fitted to her face.

'It's OK, Lisa. I'm just giving you some oxygen to help your breathing.' Kelly had to pull the mask away as the sounds her patient was making became increasingly distressed.

'Tiffany…'

Kelly could barely made sense of Lisa's words.

'She wanted the scrunchy…the one with the teddy bear… She's…she's with Chloe…'

'We're looking for them.' Kelly tried to sound reassuring. 'We've got to move you now, Lisa, and then we'll keep looking until we find the girls.'

It was a truthful promise. Rubble and debris would be removed with painstaking care by a bucket brigade until all victims had been located. Alive…or dead. It seemed a forlorn hope that anyone close to Lisa would have survived, however. There had been quite a few uninjured people at the back of the pharmacy and they would have been assisting Bob in trying to find the children. If they were alive, surely someone would have at least heard them and would have had some idea of their whereabouts.

Fletch had a collar in his hands. 'Hold her head, Kel. I'll get this on.'

Kel. Nobody had called her that since Fletch had gone from her life. She steadied Lisa's head as Fletch brushed long, blonde hair out of the way and put the collar on.

'They're bringing a scoop in. We'll use that to try and stabilise the pelvic fracture and then put her in the Stokes basket.' Fletch lifted Lisa's eyelids to shine a torch into her eyes.

'She was talking to me a minute ago.'

'She's not responsive now,' Fletch said grimly. 'We need to get moving.'

They had to pull debris out of the way to get the scoop stretcher close to their patient. Kelly put her heavy leather gloves back on over her surgical gloves to protect her hands. Broken bottles and pill containers littered the surfaces. It was just as well she had the knee pads on. The leather gloves made it impossible to refasten the stretcher clips or thread the straps through the sides but Fletch seemed to be there every time it was too awkward. They worked fast together despite the incredibly difficult environment.

Fletch shook his head as he picked up his stethoscope to check Lisa's breathing once more. Then he felt for a brachial pulse. 'It's hard to see anything properly. You did a fantastic job, getting those IVs going.'

'Thanks.' Kelly wanted to tell Fletch that he was doing an amazing job as well. That his calmness and focus were making it easy for her to do her part. That she wasn't even frightened, being in a tiny space inside a crushed building that could collapse further at any time, because he was in there with her. But she said nothing. The thoughts were only half-collected and there was no time to think about how she felt. Fire service officers were squeezing into the space to help lift the stretcher and strap it inside the basket. Kelly moved aside but not far enough. She found herself pushed by a large shoulder as a man bent to lift Lisa, and she fell sideways.

'Are you all right?' Hands were pulling her upright.

'I'm fine. Go with Lisa, Fletch.'

But he didn't move for the moment. The Stokes basket was being lifted and dragged through the hole in the pharmacy wall. Kelly rubbed her elbow and looked to see whether it had been something sharp she had landed on. Her headlamp illuminated the section of shelving her fall had displaced. There were combs and curlers and hair ties in a heap. And just underneath the edge of the shelf she could see something else.

'Come on, Kelly. Let's get out of here.'

'No—wait!' Kelly stared at the pile. 'That's a pushchair handle.' She fell back to her knees and began pulling debris towards her. She climbed over the top and tried to lift the shelf. It was too heavy.

'Help me, Fletch,' Kelly cried desperately. 'Lisa's children were in a pushchair.'

Fletch was beside her now. He stepped sideways, stumbled, cursed and then pulled himself upright again. He leaned down and pushed what looked like a metal beam that was pinning the shelf at an angle. There was a grating sound and Kelly felt the shelf move.

'It *is* a pushchair. Quick, Fletch!'

Together, they pushed harder. The shelving unit tipped and then fell with a crash.

'What's going on?' someone yelled behind them.

Neither Fletch nor Kelly responded. The pushchair had been covered with debris and the hood had been pushed down onto the occupants. They only needed to remove a little of the weight and lift the canvas hood to see that their task was hopeless.

Two little girls. One was only a baby, a few months old. The children were unmarked. Probably uninjured. They had been smothered by the canvas hood and the weight of debris. They were both dead.

'Oh, God!' Kelly put her hands over her face, unable to turn away and take the spotlight of her headlamp away from the tiny faces. She didn't need to wait for Fletch to check for any signs of life. It was all too obvious that there were none to be found.

Kelly couldn't move. Lisa had been her own age or maybe even younger. If she and Fletch had stayed together they might have had a baby by now—even a toddler. They might have looked like these children. The dream of a family had been as alive as her love for

Fletch had been once. As alive as these little girls had been only hours ago. Her own dream had been dead for a long time but two other parents had just lost their family and dreams for the future. Kelly was unaware she was crying until she felt Fletch's hands on her shoulders and her slow tears became sobs. She let him pull her away. Did he intend to pull her into a rough hug or had she initiated it? Kelly felt him hold her in his arms—just for the length of time it took another rescuer to climb towards them.

'What the—?' The rescuer saw what they had uncovered. 'Oh, jeez.' He cleared his throat. 'Your squad leader—Dave, is it? He's looking for you guys. You're being stood down for a break now. You didn't answer your radio call.'

'No.' Fletch nodded briskly as he let Kelly go. He hadn't intended to hold her like that. When he'd seen her frozen by the horror of their discovery he'd put his hands on her shoulders simply to move her away from the sight. It had been the sound of her first sob that had been his undoing.

The sound had cut him even more deeply than the tragedy they were standing beside. Kelly's pain had become his pain and the desperate need to provide comfort had been totally overwhelming. It was just as well the time to register the impact of trying to hold Kelly's distress in check had been so brief. Her grief might have sparked and then melded with the even deeper grief that Fletch kept so well buried. It had been close. Way too close. Fletch had to blink away threatened tears of his own.

'We'll head out now.' His voice was muffled enough by the dust mask to disguise the way it cracked. 'Can you deal with this?'

The acknowledgement was another determinedly brisk nod. A hand-held radio was near the man's mouth. 'We have two patients— status zero—in here. No, we can get them out without stretchers.' He had to clear his throat again. 'They're…they're just babies.'

Dave was waiting for them near the entrance to the mall. There was no sign of the other team members.

'They're stood down. You have a four-hour break. Well done, both of you.'

Kelly didn't say anything. It didn't feel like they had done well. There were two status zero children coming out behind them. They would be carried past very soon probably, and Kelly didn't want to wait long enough to see that.

'Where do we go?' she asked Dave. 'To that church hall?'

'Yes. Tony's over by the bus. He'll show you where it is. There should be a hot meal ready for you by now.'

'What I need,' Fletch said heavily, 'is a drink.'

'Sorry, mate. It won't be anything stronger than a coffee for a while yet.'

Kelly didn't wait to hear any disappointed response from Fletch. How could he even think about having a drink at a time like this? Maybe he did really 'need' one. Kelly pushed her exhausted body through the crowd milling around in the car park. She knew that Fletch was following her but she didn't want to acknowledge his company. Her reserves felt suddenly non-existent.

Tony wasn't able to give them directions immediately. A television news crew had reached him just before Kelly did.

'Where are you guys from?' he was asked.

'USAR.'

'What's that?'

'Urban Search and Rescue. We're a task force that can be deployed anywhere in the country to structural collapse or any other long-duration special incidents.'

'Cool!' A nod led to a spotlight coming on and a camera being focused on Tony. 'Mind if we get this on tape?'

'Sure.'

Kelly sighed inwardly. Maybe she should go and sit inside the bus for a few minutes to rest—but when she looked up she saw Jessica sitting in the vehicle. She looked pale and exhausted and had her eyes closed. Maybe she felt in as much need as Kelly did for a bit of personal space to try and deal with this experience. What dreadful things had Jessica seen on her hours of active duty? Kelly could only hope she hadn't had to find any children. It had been bad enough for her. Imagine how

much more traumatic it would be for a single
mother whose life was centred on her child.
Kelly couldn't tell Jessica anything about her
own experience and it was too much on her
mind to think of anything else, so it might be
better to avoid her company for a little while.

'New Zealand was part of the International
Search and Rescue Advisory group that was
formed in 1991 by the United Nations,' Tony
was telling the news crew.

Kelly had already heard the historical background of USAR. She pulled off her helmet
and turned it upside down to carry her dust
mask and goggles. She was too tired to feel
hungry any more. Or was it just that she
couldn't get the image of those children out of
her mind?

'Since then we've learned a lot from incidents such as the Oklahoma bombing, the
Threadbo landslide and that earthquake in Italy
that buried the school. Experiences like that
have led to ongoing, updated operational procedures that are part of the international SAR
response system.'

Fletch was standing beside Kelly but he wasn't listening to Tony either. 'Where's Sutherland Street?'

'I'm not sure. I think it's a dead-end street on the south side.'

'How long do you expect to be working here?' The interviewer sounded eager for more relevant information on the current disaster.

'As long as it takes to locate everybody. Alive or dead.'

'How many victims are known to be buried?'

'We don't have anything more than rough estimates.'

'How many people have been found alive so far?'

'Quite a few. Up to about twenty now, I believe.'

'How many have been found dead?'

'That's not information I could give you even if I had it.' Tony was winding up his interview. 'You'll have to get the press releases from the incident command centre like everyone else. Excuse me. We have a job to get on with here.'

Kelly watched in dismay as the camera moved and swung towards her. She didn't want to be questioned. She needed to forget about what she had just encountered—at least for a while. If she didn't, how could she prepare herself to go back inside?

'Come with me.' Fletch's calm voice was right behind her ear. 'I've found where to go. We can get a shower and some food and maybe a couple of hours' sleep.'

Gratefully, Kelly turned and followed Fletch. Tony was right. They had a job to get on with here. And it wasn't over yet.

Not by a long shot.

CHAPTER FIVE

THE church hall was crowded. Community or-
ganisations had rallied to support the emergency services working in their area.
Mattresses and pillows had been provided.
Bathroom facilities were available and a small
kitchen was pushed to maximum capacity as
hot drinks and meals were being provided.

'Four hours isn't very long,' Joe warned
Kelly, having spotted her waiting in the queue
for a meal. 'Make the most of it. Our team is
due back in soon.'

'But you went in almost the same time we
did.'

'We came out a lot earlier. You were in
there for nearly seven hours.'

'Really?' Kelly was astonished. 'I knew I'd
lost track of the time but I had no idea we were
that long.'

'You did a great job, from what I've heard.' Joe shook his head. 'We located eight people in our sector. No survivors.'

'Oh.' Kelly thought about the two little girls in the pharmacy. 'That's rough. No wonder Jessica didn't look too happy. I saw her sitting by herself in the bus.'

'She was OK until we pulled out the last two people. Then it all seemed to get too much for her suddenly. She went really pale and I thought she was going to throw up or faint or something.'

'Maybe she shouldn't go back in this time. Pamela went home before her team even got started.'

'I tried suggesting that.' Joe's smile was rueful. 'I nearly got my head bitten off. Tony had to force her to take a break at all. She was determined to carry on.'

'Has she had something to eat?'

'I don't think so.' Joe frowned. 'Maybe I'll take a sandwich back for her.'

'That's a good idea.' Kelly's appetite was making an effort to surface thanks to the smell of roast chicken wafting from the kitchen. She still wouldn't have described herself as hungry, however. 'What I really need is a shower,' she told Joe. 'I feel like that dust is ingrained in my skin. I hope my mother managed to get some clean clothes dropped off for me. I left her a message before our shift started.'

The clothes were waiting in the care of a woman supervising the bathrooms.

'Here's a towel, love. And soap. There should be a shower free in a couple of minutes.'

'Thanks.' Kelly knew the effect would be somewhat negated by having to don the same overalls and there was no point in washing her hair right now, but at least she would be clean underneath and the hot water would be as refreshing as a short nap. It was. Having finished her clean-up, Kelly bypassed the mattresses in favour of stepping outside to sit by herself for a while. Now that her immediate physical needs had been taken care of, she wanted a chance to gather mental resources. Then she would be ready for whatever was coming next. She would be ready to go back inside the mall.

Fishing her telephone from one the many pockets on the overalls, Kelly rang her mother as soon as she found a quiet spot with good reception.

'Thanks so much for bringing my stuff in, Mum.'

'Are you all right, darling? How's it going? The bits I've seen on the news look simply dreadful.'

'It is dreadful but it's good to be here trying to help, instead of just watching it. I'll tell you about it later.' Kelly knew it might take a while to want to discuss any of this with someone who wasn't as involved as she was.

'Be careful.'

'I will. How are you?'

'Oh, I'm fine. Don't you worry about me.'

Kelly caught the note in her mother's tone. 'How was the meeting? Did you tell him?'

'Not exactly.' Her mother sounded reluctant now. 'It was too hard once I saw him.'

'I knew it wasn't a good idea.'

'I couldn't do something like that in a letter or over the phone. I owe it to him, Kelly.'

'You don't owe him anything, Mum.' Kelly frowned. She felt the heavy weight of all the years of her mother supporting the family, putting up with the kind of abuse her father was capable of giving out, and all the times when she'd refused to give up on someone she had loved enough to marry. The separation enforced by her father's jail term had been the key for her mother to realise just what life had to offer. And she deserved to keep it. She couldn't really be considering taking him back now that he was due for release. She *couldn't.* 'You're not planning to see him again, are you, Mum?'

'Yes, dear. I am.'

Kelly groaned. Had she made all those phone calls, written all those letters, even given up her job to come home and support her mother during this time, only to watch her sucked back into the life she had finally escaped? 'The more time you spend with him the more likely you are to change your mind.'

'He's changed, Kelly. He says he still loves me.'

'Of course he loves you. That's his problem, not yours.'

'But he's stopped drinking. He really has this time. It's been years.'

Kelly's snort was dismissive. How many times had she heard those sincere declarations during her childhood and adolescence? 'You can't trust him, Mum. I don't care what he says. You can't trust any of them.' Her voice had risen due to the level of despair Kelly was now feeling. She looked up to ensure that her conversation was still private.

It wasn't. Neil Fletcher was leaning against the back wall of the church. He held a mug of coffee in cupped hands and he was unashamedly eavesdropping.

'I'll have to go, Mum,' Kelly said. She listened for a few seconds longer. 'So be selfish for once in your life,' she finished decisively. 'You owe it to yourself.'

Kelly met Fletch's gaze as she slipped her phone back into the pocket. She didn't expect him to apologise for listening in, not when he had never apologised for behaviour that was far less acceptable. But the words he uttered were even more unexpected than an apology.

'You astound me, Kelly Drummond. You really do.'

'Excuse me?'

'You're not content to wreck lives through your own relationships—you want other people to do the same thing.'

'What?'

'I heard you, talking to your mother. Trying to get her to dump someone.'

'You have no idea what you heard. And it's none of your business.'

'Maybe it is. It explains a few things, anyway.' Fletch sipped his coffee. 'Funny, I never realised you were such a man-hater.'

Kelly gaped at him. *'What?'* The repetition carried even stronger tones of incredulity.

'"You can't trust any of them",' Fletch mimicked. '"You don't owe him anything." Never mind that he's in love with her. That's *his* problem, isn't it? Not hers.' Fletch tossed the remains of his coffee onto the nearby shrubbery. 'You're a cold-hearted and ruthless person, do you know that, Kelly? Quite frankly, I can't understand how I could ever have fallen in love with you.'

Kelly was shocked. Really shocked. She could feel that horrible pins and needles sensation again. He didn't really believe that, did he? How could he believe that? Hadn't he held in her in his arms while she tried to cope with the grief of finding those children? Would someone cold-hearted and ruthless have been so affected?

'You're certainly the best person to advise other people to be selfish,' Fletch continued remorselessly. 'You're the expert in that field as well, aren't you?' His tone was disgusted. 'You don't really give a damn about anyone else.' Fletch turned away but then he paused. 'What made you come back, Kelly? Was it a planned move or just another spur-of-the-moment thing?' He didn't leave enough time for Kelly to respond even if she could have found any words. 'Have you left some poor bloke in Melbourne wondering just what the hell he did that was so wrong?'

'I... It's...' Kelly was shocked again. Not so much by the personal attack as by the raw strength of Fletch's anger.

'I wouldn't worry about it too much if you did,' Fletch said scathingly. He didn't turn back this time. 'He'll probably come to the conclusion that you've done him a favour.'

Like Fletch had done?

Kelly stood by herself for a long time after being left alone. Fletch's low opinion of her was humiliating. And unjustified. It wasn't as if she'd even wanted to come back to Christchurch and her reasons for doing so had been far from selfish. She didn't hate all men. And nobody had ever suggested she was cold-hearted. It was all so ironic. Kelly had come back for the same kind of reasons she had left in the first place: to protect someone from a life ruined by the misery that someone out of control could cause. The same kind of reasons that had made her flee her relationship with Neil Fletcher.

Maybe it was time he knew the truth. The guilt by association Kelly had been so ashamed of had left her past unknown to most people. Her upbringing and half her parentage had been something to bury and move on from. But maybe that desire had always been a pipe dream. Her mother was being sucked in again so what had made Kelly so confident that she could escape?

As far as gathering strength for another shift went, Kelly's break had been a miserable failure, thanks to Fletch. She pulled on her personal protection gear feeling defeated already. She attended a briefing update and listened to the grim statistics with a passive acceptance. Twenty-six fatalities had now been confirmed, including eight children. Four more people had critical injuries and were not expected to survive, including Lisa, the mother of the two little girls. Anywhere between ten and thirty people were estimated to still be missing. No new survivors had been found for the last three hours but the rescuers were encouraged not to give up hope.

'Just remember,' they were told, 'how long people have been known to survive buried under debris. In the 1976 Terngshan China

Earthquake, four hundred and fifty-nine people were rescued alive after five days.'

The adrenaline associated with the novelty of the rescue situation had worn off by the end of the first hour of Kelly's second shift. They were into a hard slog of trying to locate people buried deeply within the debris. A wire bucket brigade was now in full swing, removing small rubble. Heavy equipment was being deployed and a bobcat was busy clearing larger rubble from areas inside the mall. An elevated platform was being positioned and hydraulic jacks were operating constantly. Light towers had been set up to illuminate large areas and there were people everywhere. Fibre-optic and thermal-imaging cameras and other high-tech gear was being used. The sounds of chainsaws, concrete cutters and air hammers competed for precedence. It was crowded, dirty and noisy.

Kelly's team was deployed near the central area of damage now, amidst the wreckage of the supermarket where remnants of foodstuffs like cereal and flour made the dust even thicker. Whistle blasts for silence were often only partially successful and Kelly wondered how they could ever be expected to hear a weak survivor calling for help. Not that it seemed likely they would find any survivors in this sector. The only human remains in evidence would have to be identified by forensic means.

Despite the small number in their squad, Kelly managed to stay clear of Fletch. Or was he staying clear of her? It didn't matter. The net result was the same and Kelly felt her spirits falling steadily.

'Owen? Over here.' Kelly waited until he got close before indicating where the marking was needed. Owen's face was set in grim lines as he sprayed another orange 'V' and put a line through it. There was another team to collect the dead, or parts thereof. Kelly's team was there to locate and rescue the living, if possible.

Dave called them together a short time later. 'We've been cleared to start a new sector. Someone thinks they heard someone calling.'

They passed another USAR team as they moved. Kelly could see Joe having what appeared to be an argument with another man, but she couldn't make out any of what was being said because of the background noise. Then she saw Jessica standing well behind Joe. A police officer was holding her arm as though keeping her detained, and Jessica looked upset. Kelly skipped a step or two and touched Dave's arm. He turned to observe the scene she indicated. Frowning, he shook his head in response to Kelly's questioning gaze.

'I've no idea what's going on,' he told her. 'I'm sure we'll find out soon enough.'

They started their new search in a section of the mall on the other side of the supermarket, working back towards where they had been. The lift shaft and stairwell that led down to the car park was on this side and it was near the stairwell that someone thought they had heard a voice. They checked through the shops bordering the damaged area first. It was possible that someone had been missed on the initial search.

'Rescue team here. Can anyone hear me?'

Dave could hear his radio message. He used another channel to contact Tony. Kelly was close enough to overhear the conversation and the expression on both their faces by the time he signed off the communication was enough to prompt Fletch to approach them.

'What's going on?'

'It's Jessica,' Dave told him. 'Apparently her mother was amongst the last fatalities her team located.'

'My God,' Fletch said in horror. 'Has she just found out?'

'No.' Dave looked grim. 'She recognised her mother at the time. She just didn't tell anybody.'

'Why on earth not?'

'Because her son was with her mother and he's still missing. She knew if she told someone they would stop her searching.'

'So she's still in here?' Fletch still sounded horrified.

'Joe's been trying to persuade people to let her continue.' Dave shook his head. 'Tony's had to step in. She can't be allowed to carry on searching.'

'Why not?' Kelly asked.

'She's in no fit state to act rationally. She won't hesitate to put herself in danger if she thinks she can get to her son. She may endanger other team members.'

'This is awful.' Kelly didn't want to try and calculate the long odds of Jessica's son still being alive.

'There might be some unidentified children amongst the injured,' Fletch suggested. 'Maybe he got taken out earlier.'

'Let's hope so.' Dave turned away at a shout from one of the team.

'I think I heard something. Over here.'

It took twenty minutes to locate the origin of the weak, intermittent sound. A cubicle in a toilet block had remained intact enough to protect its inhabitant. The older woman was shocked and very short of breath. Her asthma had been exacerbated by the dust, her Ventolin inhaler had run out and she had been too terrified to leave the safety of the cubicle to seek rescue.

'We're going to get you out now, Jan. You're going to be fine.' Kelly tried to keep up her level of reassurance as she sorted supplies to set up an IV line.

'We'll try some IV adrenaline,' Fletch decided, 'and get moving as soon as they get in with the portable oxygen and stretcher.'

It was not an easy job to locate and then cannulate a suitable vein in the woman's arm. Kelly bit her lip as she advanced the needle. She did not want to fail. Their patient needed medication to deal with her increasing respiratory distress. The fact that Fletch was watching made failure even less acceptable. Kelly breathed a sigh of relief as she slid the cannula into place. She released the tourniquet and tamponaded the end of the cannula, ready to remove the needle casing and cap the end of the IV access line. As she attached the luer plug and started to tighten it, a loud noise made her patient cry out in fright. Kelly caught the fear instantly. The sound was too loud to be part of the background noise they had become accustomed to. It was loud enough to shake the walls and provoke a rain of new dust and small pieces of rubble.

'Oh, my God, it's coming down.' Had both Kelly and Fletch been too intent on patient care to watch for any signs of secondary collapse in the area?

The three short whistle blasts from their squad leader, signalling the need to evacuate, only increased Kelly's fear, sending it spiralling into panic. She stood up hurriedly, the contents of her bum bag spilling into the dust. Fletch leaned past her. He calmly tightened the now leaking luer plug and put a piece of tape over the cannula hub to hold it in place.

'Where's the adrenaline?'

'We have to get out, Fletch. There's no time.'

Kelly was rewarded with an impatient glance. Fletch looked at the debris around her feet now littered with her medical supplies. The capped syringe of adrenaline he had drawn up and put with Kelly's supplies ready for administration was now lying half-buried beneath IV cannula and dressing packages. He plucked the syringe free, injected the drug and then scooped up their patient.

'Let's go, then.'

Kelly was left following in the wake of Fletch's long strides. The new shower of debris had stopped but Kelly was still terrified that a further collapse was imminent. Had Fletch not been frightened or had he simply put the needs of his patient ahead of his own fear? Maybe he would chalk up another score against Kelly for being selfish enough to want to get out without taking the extra seconds to administer what could prove to be a life-saving drug for their patient. Kelly didn't care. She just wanted to get out.

The evacuation had been wide-spread and there was a huge crowd outside the main entrance. Excited queries and speculation abounded and Kelly overheard parts of three separate conversations as she followed both Fletch and Dave towards the ambulance triage station.

'What's going on?'
'There was another explosion.'
'Was anybody hurt?'
'Don't know. Haven't heard a thing.'

'What the hell was it?'
'There's a shop that sells barbecues. They

have a supply of compressed gas cylinders. Someone reckons it might have been a damaged LPG cylinder that went off.'

'Didn't it cause another wall to come down?'

'Part of the basement car park ceiling went.'

'Some guy went running into the car park as it was coming down.'

'What the hell did he do that for?'

'Heaven knows. I went in the opposite direction as fast I could. I thought the whole lot was on the way down.'

'Someone reckons they saw a kid—in the car park.'

'Really? Alive?'

'Apparently. Anyway, this guy in blue overalls goes diving in just after they've said it's not safe, and *bang*! The ceiling comes down.'

'Who was he?'

'Dunno. Who wears those blue overalls and the helmets and goggles and stuff?'

'I think it's USAR. He should have known better. Is he OK?'

'Doubt it. No way of finding out now. It's completely blocked off.'

Kelly pulled at Dave's arm. 'Did you hear that?'

'Yeah.'

'They're talking about Jessica, aren't they? She thinks Ricky was in the car park and she went in after him.' A bystander wouldn't be able to distinguish the sex of a USAR worker from any distance. The 'guy' had to be Jessica. One of her classmates. A friend.

'We'll find out,' Dave promised. 'Look!' He pointed ahead. 'That's Jessica over there, isn't it?'

It was. Kelly left Fletch to transfer the care of their patient to the ambulance service just ahead in the triage tent. She changed directed instantly and moved swiftly. She ignored the police officers surrounding Jessica.

'Jess! Are you OK?'

'Oh, Kelly!' Jessica reached out and Kelly pulled her into a tight hug.

'I heard about your mother. About Ricky,' she said. 'God, Jess! Someone said they saw you run into the car park—that you were trapped. I'm so glad it's not true.'

'But it is,' Jessica sobbed. 'Ricky's in there. In the car park.'

'Joe stopped Jessica going in after him.' Kelly hadn't seen Tony standing close to Jessica. 'He knew how dangerous it was.'

'He went in himself instead.' June was alongside Jessica as well. 'Nobody thought to try stopping him.'

'And then it was too late,' Tony added grimly. 'The explosion happened and the ceiling came down right beside us. We had to run for our lives.'

Kelly held Jessica tightly. She could feel the distraught trembling which was now the only indication of what Jessica was going through. The crying had stopped. Jessica pulled free of Kelly's embrace.

'We have to go back in,' she said matter-of-factly. 'We have to find them.'

'We'll go back as soon as it's cleared for safety,' Tony said. 'But not you this time, Jessica. You'll have to leave this search for us.'

'It's my fault that Joe's in trouble. I have to help.'

'The best help you can give is to look after yourself right now. You need to be away from here for a while. Kelly or June can take you over to the church hall and look after you.'

'No. I want to stay here. My son is in there, Tony. He…' Jessica choked back a sob. 'He might still be alive.'

'You can stay close,' Tony decided. 'But you can't come back inside.'

'But—'

'It's OK, Jess,' Kelly said firmly. 'You can rely on us.'

'It's going to be a while before they let any of us back in.' Dave had joined the small group now and Fletch was close behind him. 'We don't know how major this secondary collapse is yet. Take Jessica back to the hall, Kelly. Have some time out yourself.'

'No.' Kelly didn't want to go now either. Any thought that she didn't want to go back into the mall herself had been banished. This rescue had just become far too personal. 'I'm staying. I want to be ready when they call for us.'

'It could be a while. At least go and grab a drink and some food. You need to keep your fluids up or you won't be able to keep going.'

It was sensible. Everybody was sent over to the church hall and Kelly was part of quite a large group for the five-minute walk to Sutherland Street. She stayed away from Fletch. How dared he accuse her of being cold-hearted and selfish? He didn't know her at all. One of these days he would find out just how wrong he was. He might find out just how hard it had been to do what she had done. Cold hearts didn't break. And selfish people didn't care this much about what happened to their friends and colleagues.

Kelly was walking with one arm around Jessica.

'Joe will have found Ricky,' she told her. 'I'm sure of it. And if there's any way he can keep them both safe then he'll do it. He's not a helicopter paramedic for nothing. Joe's coped with some pretty dodgy situations in his time—even a chopper crash once.'

'I can't lose them both.' Jessica was deathly pale. 'Not Mum *and* Ricky. Especially not Ricky.' The last words were a whisper. 'He's my whole life.'

'I know.' One day Kelly might find out what it was like to be a mother but she wouldn't want to do it all by herself, to have her entire world centred on one person. She would want a father for that child. A partner who would be her strength in times of crisis. A dimension in her life of equal importance.

'Is there anyone we can contact for you, Jess?' Fletch had moved so that he was walking closer to the two women. 'Any family or friends from home?'

'No. The only people that matter are here. Mum…and Ricky.'

They had passed the incident command centre and the ambulance triage station. They all knew what lay in the tent behind the ambulance loading slot.

'I want to go in there,' Jessica said quietly. 'I want to see Mum again.'

'Are you sure?' Kelly's eyes prickled with the threat of tears as she glanced towards the temporary morgue the tent contained.

Jessica just nodded. She cleared her throat. 'Would you come with me, please, Kelly?'

'I...' Kelly had to swallow the lump in her throat. She knew how hard that would be.

'I'll come with you, Jess.' It was Fletch who made the offer.

Kelly caught his gaze. What was he trying to do? Prove that he was more caring than she was?

'I...I just want Kelly to come.' Jessica was crying again. 'Please, Kelly?'

'Of course I will.' Kelly's glance dismissed Fletch. 'We'll get through this together, Jess.'

Somehow, they did. Maybe Jessica was too absorbed by her fear for Ricky to take in the grief of losing her mother just yet. Kelly knew her friend was in for a rough time over the next few months. She hoped, desperately, that a miracle would happen and her son would survive.

It was half an hour later that Kelly turned up at the church hall. She found a cup of sweet tea for Jessica and left her friend for a minute to make what had become an extremely urgent trip to the toilet. Jessica was wrapped in a blanket and sitting on a mattress surrounded by supportive classmates with June and Wendy on either side of her.

The toilet facilities were unisex by necessity. The doors on the cubicles all showed an engaged flag except for one that was halfway between engaged and vacant. Kelly knocked.

'Anyone in there?'

'Yes.'

The tone was abrupt and the voice came from a person whose back Kelly could already see thanks to the fact that her knock had been enough to make the door swing inwards. The occupant of the stall was standing. He turned to shove the door closed again and the action was so hurried that he was in view for only a split second, but it was quite long enough for Kelly to recognise him.

Neil Fletcher.

'It's all yours.' The occupant of another cubicle emerged behind Kelly.

'Thanks.' Kelly went in and locked the door behind her but, despite the urgency of her mission, she didn't move for several seconds. She leaned against the door.

She couldn't have seen what she thought she'd seen. It made no sense. What could Fletch be doing with a hypodermic syringe in his hand?

It made perfect sense if Kelly was going to allow her mind to go there. She knew Fletch had had a problem but she'd assumed it had only involved alcohol. Maybe that had just been the tip of an iceberg. All doctors had the opportunity to get into heavier drugs. Had Fletch just travelled further down the road of dependency or had she really not known him as well as she thought she had? At least it wasn't her problem any longer. Not on a personal level.

On a professional level, however, Kelly was very much involved. So was everybody who had anything to do with Dr Fletcher—colleagues and patients alike. Kelly had a responsibility here but she knew what would happen if she did what was ethically essential. By exposing him she would totally destroy the life of a man she had once loved.

Could she live with herself if she did that?

Could she live with herself if she *didn't* do that?

CHAPTER SIX

NOTHING needed to be done just yet.

It was possible that Kelly had made a mistake. Not about the syringe. There was no denying the fact that Fletch had been holding it, but there could be a plausible explanation. Maybe Fletch had decided to take a moment to tidy the bum bag he was wearing, having had to remove it to take his overalls off. Had he drawn up a second dose of adrenaline for their patient that he hadn't needed to use? Or had the syringe been the empty one? There was really no need to jump to conclusions or involve anyone else at this point. Kelly just needed to be watchful, to take her time over such a disturbing issue.

How much time was irrelevant because the position of clock hands had lost any meaning. Daylight hours had come and gone and the transition had barely been registered. They were into the second day of this incident now and hope of finding any more survivors was fading. Relays of grim-faced and exhausted rescuers kept going. Respite had been inadequate with any real rest elusive, but they had no intention of stopping. Thanks to the media picking up the story about Joe and Ricky, the entire nation was waiting for news—waiting to see if, by some miracle, the heroic paramedic and the disabled child would be found alive.

USAR technicians had flown in from the north island now and many tired team members had been replaced. June had opted out of any further duties and both Owen and Roger had been stood down. Kyle had refused replacement.

'No way, man. I'm not missing this.'

Kelly wished she had even a fraction of Kyle's seemingly unquenchable enthusiasm. She found herself stealing glances at the young volunteer firefighter during the briefing that had become just another part of the routine. Kyle was listening eagerly to the statistics. The number of dead and seriously injured had crept up only a little. The number of people unaccounted for had dropped markedly. Areas of damage in the supermarket had been carefully mapped now with fewer no-go sections. The suggestion that the explosion had not been an accident was gaining credence and new teams of police forensic experts were starting work to examine the disaster area for evidence.

Kelly waited for the separate USAR briefing, wishing she had had a replacement urged on her, but no offers had been made to herself, Wendy, Fletch or Ross. Medics with their qualifications were a rare commodity.

'How's it going, Ross?' Kelly could see the lines of strain on the young doctor's face, and he would have to be the most physically fit of their whole class, with the possible exception of Wendy. Kelly was grateful she hadn't been near a mirror in the last twenty-four hours. If Ross looked this weary and grubby, she hated to imagine what she must look like.

'I'm stuffed,' Ross confessed. 'How 'bout you?'

'I'll be very glad to go home,' Kelly responded. 'If it wasn't for the fact that Joe's still trapped in there, I'm not sure I'd want to face any more of this.'

'It's a lot tougher than I thought it would be. Pretty horrendous, in fact, isn't it?'

Kelly just nodded. She could see the incident command officers conferring. Any moment now they would receive the instructions for their next tour of duty. 'Do you think he's still alive, Ross?' Kelly had to ask. She badly needed some reassurance.

'I don't know.' The sigh was heartfelt. 'I hope so.'

'Me, too.' Kelly was now watching Kyle again, who was flicking his headlamp on and off. The flashing of the light on the tent wall was irritating. 'Has he been this hyped all the time?'

'Pretty much. I'd like to know where he finds the energy.' Ross looked as though he was sharing Kelly's irritation. 'He's never used the breaks to rest. He sneaks back to watch what's going on. He was even in the morgue the last time we chased him up.'

'Good grief.' Kelly couldn't imagine going into that particular tent unless it was absolutely necessary. She wouldn't forget her visit there with Jessica in a hurry.

Wendy had had enough of Kyle's method of passing the time. 'Turn it off, Kyle,' she snapped. 'Or on. Just make up your mind, for heaven's sake. You're driving me nuts.'

'Oh, sorry.' Kyle flicked his lamp off and smiled at Wendy. 'How long do you think this is going to take?'

'I have no idea, Kyle. We'll have to keep looking until everybody is located. It might take days yet.'

'No, I meant how long before we can go back inside?'

Wendy simply shook her head and Kelly felt herself smiling sympathetically. Kyle's eagerness was not shared by anyone other than fresh recruits, and the answer would come soon enough anyway. It was Dave who addressed the waiting USAR personnel.

'USAR 2 is going to work from the base on the Desmond Street entrance. A crane is being used to clear the car park exit at that point. At least two vehicles are known to have been caught on the outward ramp.

'USAR 4 is going to level 2, starting on the south side.' Dave's pointer traced a circle around the area on the map. 'Your squad leader will now be Tony.'

A significant glance was exchanged between several listeners. Tony had been leading USAR 3 but the team had virtually disintegrated. June had gone home. Jessica was not allowed to return to duty and Joe... The fate of USAR 3's other medic was on everybody's mind.

'USAR 5 is coming inside again with me,' Dave continued. 'We're going to try an approach to the car park area from the fire escape next to Toyland.' He tapped another location on the map. 'Getting to that point through the remaining section of the pharmacy looks like a possibility. We'll be working under the section being covered by USAR 4 so we'll keep in close radio contact to share information.'

Dave looked around the silent group. 'We're into the second day now so biological hazards are increasing. There are bodies that haven't been located, sewerage systems have been disrupted and oxygen levels will be further reduced. Pockets of gas are still likely. Don't

enter any new void until the atmospheric testing has been done.'

There was no other option than to go
through the pharmacy again, with the heart-
wrenching reminder of finding those two little
girls. Kelly followed her team members silently as they returned to a scene that was not
losing any of its nightmarish qualities due to
familiarity. Even if this shopping precinct was
completely restored, Kelly was not sure she
would ever want to set foot on its tiled walkways again.

Large quantities of debris had been shifted
now. It was easy to gain access to the pharmacy and beyond. The supermarket had been
searched as far as possible and many victims
removed. Kelly's team was now being deployed to one side of the worst-hit area adjacent to where the second floor had collapsed.
Reinforced concrete drooped like badly hung
wallpaper, with lengths of steel rod poking like
fingers into huge gaps. Voids beneath slabs of
concrete had to be checked. The debris took
on a new horror for Kelly when they neared
the toy shop. Soft toys and dolls lay dusty and

ruined. Plastic building bricks crunched under steel-capped boots. This was the place they were most likely to find more children. Kelly had to clear her throat more than once to be able to raise her voice.

'Rescue team here. Can you hear me?'

Nothing. Again and again silence was ordered and the team went through its drill, moving slowly forward, a metre at a time. Minutes crawled into hours and Kelly wondered if she would ever breathe again without smelling stale air filtered from thick dust or be able to blink without the discomfort of gritty, sore eyes. Surely it would all be over soon.

Dave was keeping in close touch with Tony and USAR 4. They were still overhead, having searched a large area on level 2, and were now reaching their limit where the damaged flooring made it unsafe to go close. There had been a couple of false hopes. Kyle was sure he had heard someone calling. Tony and other team members couldn't confirm his belief but they had to be sure before they gave up.

Silence was called for throughout the site. Kelly's team stopped and waited. The call for silence filtered back and pneumatic equipment was shut down. Wheelbarrows were halted. A bucket brigade put down their wire rubble baskets. They all waited. Kelly could hear the calls coming from above.

'Rescue team here. Can you hear me?'

Silence.

And then a shout. A loud shout. Almost a scream. Dave's radio buzzed a second later.

'Dave? We've got a problem.'

'What's up, Tony?'

'Kyle's got himself in trouble. He went out on his own and he's stepped onto a single piece of reinforcing rod. He's impaled his leg.'

They could all hear Kyle screaming.

'He's close to an edge. Can you see him from where you are?'

They were all looking up towards the source of the dreadful sound. A dim shape could be seen writhing in the shadows of the upper level.

'Help! Someone *help* me!'

A figure moved past Kelly to get closer to the gap in the ceiling. 'Have we got some sort of ladder or platform we can get in here?'

Fletch was staring upwards. 'We might be able to reach him.'

'It's nearly five metres.' Dave changed the channel on his radio. 'Let's find out what might be available.'

The calls for help became more frantic. Tony's voice was hard to hear over the sound of Kyle's voice when he responded to Dave's message that a ladder was on its way.

'We've got a bit closer. It looks stable enough if we're careful.'

'Can you cut the reinforcing rod and get him free that way?'

'Might have to. Ross is going to try and have a look at his leg.'

They were all watching as Ross slowly approached Kyle, his headlamp illuminating the scene. They could see Ross bending towards Kyle's leg. And they all saw Kyle grab the medic's arm.

'Don't touch my leg, man! It *hurts*!'

Did Kyle push him away or did Ross lose his balance and then his carefully calculated footing? Kelly couldn't believe what she was watching. Ross didn't have a hope of saving himself. He was propelled towards the edge and fell with a spiralling movement to land with a sickening thud a split second later on the broken concrete slabs only metres away from where Fletch was standing. He lay on his back with a deathly stillness.

For another second nobody moved. The silence was more complete than it had been during any of their rescue calls. Even Kyle stopped screaming as the horror of what had just happened registered. It was Fletch who broke the stunned immobility of the scene. He stepped forward and crouched beside Ross.

'Ross. Can you hear me, mate?'

Kelly stumbled towards them. She could see Ross's eyes flicker open. He was conscious. Was it even remotely possible that he could have escaped serious injury?

'Can you hear me, Ross?' Fletch sounded calm. 'Do you know where you are?'

The dust mask had been pulled clear. Ross's lips moved but no sound came out.

Kelly crouched beside Fletch. 'Is his airway clear?'

Fletch had his hands on either side of Ross's face now, supporting his neck as he pushed the jaw forward to ensure an open airway. 'He's breathing.'

Ross opened his eyes again and groaned.

'It's OK, Ross,' Kelly said. 'You've had a fall. Don't try and move until we've checked you out.'

'Can't...move.'

'What can't you move, mate?' Fletch was still holding Ross's head.

'Legs...' The power of speech was returning to Ross. 'I can't...feel...my legs.'

'Squeeze my hands, Ross.' Kelly pulled the leather glove and put her fingers into his palm. Her glance at Fletch and the tiny shake of her head confirmed what he could see for himself. The hand made only a flicker of movement.

'Does anything hurt, Ross?'

'My neck. God, Fletch, I've broken my bloody neck, haven't I?'

'Don't jump to conclusions,' Fletch told him. 'You've certainly done something and we're going to make damned sure we take care of you until you've been checked out properly.' He looked up. 'Grab a C-collar, will you, Kelly? Dave—come and shift some of this rubbish so we can get Ross lying on a more even surface.'

'I've broken my neck.' Ross sounded almost surprised. 'I'm still breathing so I guess it's lower than C5.'

'Just keep as still as you can.' Fletch was concentrating on supporting Ross's head as other team members carefully moved some smaller pieces of rubble from around and beneath Ross.

Medical back-up had been urgently summoned. A Stokes basket arrived with a backboard and collar included in the supplies it contained.

'We'll ease the helmet off,' Fletch instructed. 'I'll hold his head. You undo the strap and get it clear, Kelly.'

She had to work around Fletch's hands, needing to gently ease the ends of the straps clear of his fingers without allowing any movement of Ross's head. Then she had to wiggle the helmet clear, a fraction of an inch at a time.

'Slow down,' Fletch ordered. 'Try and be a bit more careful, Kelly.'

Kelly bit back the retort that she was being as careful as humanly possible. She was making damned sure she didn't do anything to invite criticism. Not because Fletch was watching like a hawk but because this was Ross. And this terrible accident should never have happened.

With the helmet and dust mask completely removed, it was possible for Kelly to check for obvious injuries to the neck area.

'Trachea's midline,' she told Fletch.

'I can see that for myself.'

Kelly ignored the tone. Fletch was probably as upset as she was that this had happened to a friend. She carefully slid her fingers beneath Ross's neck to feel the top of his spine.

'No obvious deformity,' she informed Fletch. 'Pain is over C6 to C8.'

It wasn't until they had the neck collar on and an oxygen mask in place that Kelly realised how quiet it still was around them. People were just standing and watching and the atmosphere was one of deep dismay. One of their number was injured and, from the way the medical team was acting, it didn't look good.

'What's the blood pressure?'

'105 over 68.' Kelly still had her hand on Ross's wrist. 'Heart rate's 120.'

'It's about time you had an IV line in. What gauge cannula are you going to use?'

'Fourteen.' If Fletch criticised her choice or technique, she would suggest that he let someone else support the alignment of Ross's spine so that he could do it himself. Happily, the procedure was easy and swift.

'Any signs of other trauma?' Fletch wasn't going to allow Kelly even a moment's respite.

Having already started a rapid survey, Kelly found the query unnecessary. She was just as keen as Fletch was to do this job to the best of her ability. 'Chest clear,' she said without glancing up. 'Diaphragmatic breathing.' She continued her examination, interspersed with minimal summaries. 'Abdo soft. Pelvis stable. Abrasions to left thigh. No fracture.' She tested the neurological deficit and passed on the findings with disquiet. 'Paresthesia in all limbs. Paresis in both arms and paralysis of both legs.' How much of it would be permanent was impossible to guess.

They positioned the backboard and extra people were summoned for a log roll. Kelly quickly felt down the knobs of the vertebrae when Ross had been tipped carefully sideways to allow the backboard to be slid into place.

'Get on with it, Kelly.' Fletch sounded frankly irritable now. 'I want to get Ross immobilised a bit better than this.'

'No obvious deformities.' Kelly's tone was clipped. It wouldn't be helping Ross to hear the tension Fletch was taking out on her. Not that Ross seemed aware of it. Wendy had made her way to the scene from the upper level now and was crouched as close as she could get to Ross. She held one of his hands tightly gripped between her own and was talking to him with quiet reassurance. 'There's a lot of bruising and abrasions,' Kelly continued. 'With tenderness at about T4 and T10 and L4 to 5.'

'OK. We'll lower onto the backboard on the count of three.' Fletch was still holding Ross's head carefully. 'One, two…three.'

The padded cushions of the head immobiliser were positioned.

'Get some padding under his neck and lumbar region,' Fletch ordered. 'And get those straps fastened. Have you taken any hard objects out of his pockets?'

'Not yet.'

'Perhaps you could manage that, Dave. Car keys, shears, torch—anything like that.'

Kelly ignored the implied criticism that it was a task she should have already managed. She knew it was important to remove anything that could cause a pressure injury but she hadn't exactly been wasting her time. It had been less than ten minutes since the accident and Ross had been assessed, had IV access, was receiving oxygen and was ready to immobilise and transport. Given the circumstances they were working under, they were doing extremely well.

Kelly clipped the body straps onto each side of the backboard. 'Cross it over and then thread it through the handle on your side,' she instructed Dave. 'Then pass it back to me.'

The straps got tangled as it came back to Kelly's side. She fumbled to straighten them and get the ends clipped together.

'For God's sake, Kelly, you're supposed to know what you're doing.' Fletch reached for the fastening clip.

'I do,' Kelly shot back. She yanked the strap free of Fletch's grip. Wendy had given Fletch a surprised stare. Did he not realise that his bad temper was making this situation even worse?

Finally, they had Ross securely strapped. There were plenty of hands available to lift the backboard and place it gently inside the Stokes basket.

'OK, Ross, we're moving now, mate.' Fletch wiped perspiration-streaked dust from his forehead. 'We'll get you into Emergency in no time and sort this out.'

'Hope there's someone on duty who knows what they're doing.'

'There will be,' Fletch promised. The smile he gave Ross was the first Kelly had seen on his face in a very long while. 'Me.'

So this was it, then. Kelly followed the team carrying Ross, picking her way through the rubble. Fletch was going. By the time he'd seen Ross through his initial assessment and treatment, this whole incident would probably be over. There wasn't much left for USAR team members to do here anyway. Kelly would probably be sent home soon enough and she was ready to go. This had become a very personal disaster. She had made some good friends over the last three weeks and in the space of two days lives she was involved with had been shattered. The trauma of dealing with their first USAR call-out and the tragedy of so many lives being lost would have been enough for any of them to deal with. On top of that, Jessica had lost her mother and probably her son. Ross was badly injured, which would affect Wendy almost as much as him. And Joe... Kelly tried to push back threatening tears. She focused on Fletch's back as he walked ahead of her to one side of the basket stretcher.

Was it her imagination or was Fletch having more trouble than she was, negotiating the uneven terrain? Kelly had almost forgotten she was watching out for signs of drug dependency. Had Fletch's irritation been purely the result of the added tension the identity of their patient had created, or could it have something to do with withdrawal symptoms? Kelly's suspicions sharpened as Fletch gave a lurch sideways that was obvious enough to attract Dave's attention.

'You OK, mate?'

'I'm fine.' The response was curt.

'Watch your feet, then,' Dave grinned as he shook his head. 'You look like you've had one too many.'

Kelly could feel a chill tracing the length of her spine. Yes. That was exactly how Fletch looked. Intoxicated. But she'd been with him for hours and he'd drunk nothing other than the water in the bottle he carried. Or was it water? Vodka wouldn't look any different, would it? Maybe Fletch had used the encouragement they all received to stay hydrated to keep himself topped up with something a little stronger. The memory of what Kelly had seen in the toilets flashed back repeatedly like some kind of subliminal message. She sighed miserably. Add that issue to the list of personal disasters she had stepped into by joining this group.

There was an expectant small crowd in the main mall near the entrance.

'They've found Joe,' someone called out to them. 'And the kid.'

'Really?' Surely people wouldn't be looking this excited if the news wasn't good?

'They got themselves into a furniture van in the car park. They're safe.'

'Are they injured?'

'Apparently not. They're just breaking through to the space they're in now. They should be out any minute.'

'You should see the media waiting for them outside!'

Even Ross was smiling as much as he was capable of with the neck collar holding his jaw and his face half-covered with the oxygen mask. They kept moving. It *was* good news. Great news. Fletch wasn't smiling, however. He had dropped further away from the procession carrying Ross and he became separated as they edged through the much larger crowd waiting outside the mall. TV crews, journalists and photographers made a human barrier which the authorities were having difficulty confining. Lights dazzled the emerging figures as flashbulbs went on and spotlights were re-directed.

'Is this the doctor that fell?'

'Is it true he's broken his back?'

'Can we have a few words? Is Dr Turnball able to talk?'

'No.' Dave brushed them aside. 'Make way, would you?' He caught Kelly's attention. 'Where's Fletch?'

Kelly turned her head but couldn't see him. 'I'll find him. Get Ross into triage and we'll join you in a minute.'

She pushed back through the journalists and photographers that had closed in behind their procession. Questions bounced around her ears.

'What's your name, love?'

'How far away is that helicopter chap? And the little boy?'

'Any truth in the rumour that they're both still alive?'

Kelly could see Fletch now, moving in the wrong direction to get to the ambulance triage tent. He was heading towards the buses that were the USAR base. He stopped before Kelly caught up. She could see him leaning against the side of an army truck. He had dropped his leather gloves and was staring blankly at the now retreating journalists.

'What's the matter, Fletch?'

'Nothing. Go away, Kelly.'

Kelly caught his wrist. He shook off her hand but not before she had registered the rapid pulse under her fingers and felt how clammy and cool his skin was.

'You're sick,' she stated.

Fletch shook his head. 'My health is none of your business, Kelly. Leave me alone.'

'I think it *is* my business,' Kelly retorted. 'You're needed, Fletch. Ross is expecting you to travel into Emergency with him. We're on the same team at the moment, in case you've forgotten.' She was trying to assess Fletch visually as she spoke. He was still staring past her with an almost blank expression. He was pale and she could see beads of perspiration on his forehead. 'What's more, you have a professional position in an area that is also my business. If you're putting the safety of patients in jeopardy with your health problems, I'm going to have to do something about it.'

Fletch was ignoring her. He had turned and was continuing to walk towards the USAR buses. Kelly followed him.

'Don't forget that I saw what you were doing in the toilets, Fletch.'

'Just clear off, Kelly.' Fletch jerked his head dismissively. 'If you get out of my face for two minutes, I'll be able to deal with this myself.'

'Oh, I'm sure you will,' Kelly said coolly.

Fletch had reached the door of the bus. It seemed an effort to pull himself up to the first step. He turned slowly. 'So? What are you waiting for?'

'I'm not going anywhere,' Kelly informed him. 'I think I should find out just how you plan to ''deal'' with this.'

Fletch snorted impatiently. 'The same way I usually do.'

Kelly followed him up the steps into the deserted bus. Her expression was incredulous.

'You're not even ashamed of yourself, are you?'

'I don't have anything to be ashamed of.'

'That's a matter of opinion. If you're not ashamed of it, why are you trying to hide?'

'I'm not.' Fletch was pulling at a carry bag he had left on the seat of the bus. 'Just go *away*, Kelly. This has nothing to do with you.'

'Yes, it does,' she contradicted. 'I'm not going to cover for you, Fletch. If you tell me to go again, I will. I'll go straight to whoever is in charge of the emergency department tonight and I'll let them know that you're incapable of doing your job without shooting up periodically.'

Fletch abandoned his attempt to open the zip fastening of the bag. He seemed to be focusing on Kelly properly for the first time. 'Shooting up?' His lips curved into a caricature of a smile. 'Just what the hell do you think I'm planning to take? Heroin?'

'Morphine's probably more easily accessible for an ED consultant.'

Fletch shook his head very slowly. He concentrated on the zip again. 'You're amazing.'

He also seemed to be concentrating on his speech. The words were apparently more of an effort to enunciate now. 'Do you think that being dumped by you would send me into the depths of drug addiction?' He had the bag open now. 'Well, I've got news for you, Kelly Drummond.' Fletch lowered himself onto the seat, clutching a small orange box. 'You wouldn't have been worth it.'

Kelly was staring at a container she recognised. 'Glucagon? You're taking *glucagon*?'

Fletch was unsuccessfully trying to open the box. 'Yep.'

Kelly took the box from his hand. 'Here, give that to me.'

'No. Give it back.'

It was simple to avoid the clutch of his hand. 'You're not co-ordinated enough to do this for yourself. I'm not even sure you should be doing it. Have you tested your blood-glucose level?'

'I don't need to. I've lived with this long enough to know what I need. Give me the bloody syringe.'

'Roll up your sleeve.' Kelly was quite prepared to believe Fletch. He certainly had all
the signs of being hypoglycaemic. She quickly
filled the syringe with the ampoule of water
provided to mix with the powder it contained,
swabbed the skin on his upper arm, flattened
the skin, inserted the needle and injected its
contents.

'I've got jellybeans in here.' Fletch was
pulling his bum bag to one side. 'I'll be able
to eat them in a few minutes without throwing
up.'

Kelly's radio crackled. She picked it up and
identified herself.

'Kelly, where are you? Where's Fletch?
They're ready to load Ross here.'

'Give us five minutes,' Kelly responded.
'We'll be there.' She looked at Fletch. 'Why
did you never tell me you were a diabetic,
Fletch?'

'You weren't around to tell.'

She had been, though. He could have told
her at any time during the three months of their
intense relationship. But, then, she'd had
things she hadn't told Fletch, hadn't she? Was

his illness something he had been ashamed of?
She took a deep breath.

'The last time I saw you—two years ago—
when we went out to dinner? When I thought
you were terribly drunk? You were hypo then,
weren't you?'

Fletch shrugged. 'Maybe. I don't know.'

'What do you mean, you don't know?'

'I have a vague memory that we were going
out somewhere. Or planning to go out somewhere. But I didn't remember anything and
there was no one around who could tell me.'

'We went out to dinner.' Kelly stared at
Fletch as she spoke, trying to determine
whether he was telling the truth. 'You chose
that really expensive restaurant because you
said we had to celebrate the one-month anni-
versary of our engagement. You ordered a
whole bottle of champagne even though you
knew I wouldn't drink any of it.' Kelly turned
away. 'We'd better go, Fletch. They're waiting
for us. Ross needs you.'

'Wait.' Fletch was staring at Kelly now. He
was clearly focused again. The glucagon and
the jellybeans were having a rapid effect. 'You

know the answers. The gap between when life was everything I wanted and when it fell apart. I need to know, Kelly. I *have* to know.'

'There isn't much to know.' Kelly knew that Fletch was following her as she led the way from the privacy of the bus. 'We went out. You got very drunk, or so everybody thought. We had an argument and there was a scene in the restaurant.'

'What kind of scene?'

'Kelly? Where the hell are you?'

She pushed the button on her radio. 'Almost there, Dave.' Kelly shook her head slightly. 'I ordered a taxi for you, Fletch. I tried to ring you the next day and your flatmate said you were sick. I wasn't surprised.'

'You thought I had a hangover.' Fletch was nodding as though a puzzle was being solved.

Kelly returned the nod. They were passing the incident command trucks now. She could see the ambulance beside the triage tent, its beacons flashing. The back doors were open and Wendy was sitting on one stretcher, her arm extended as she held Ross's hand. An ambulance officer was standing by the back doors, waiting for Fletch. He held the signs that would be slotted across the doors when they were shut to indicate the transfer of an unstable spinal injury patient. SLOW TRANSPORT. PASS WITH CARE.

Kelly's steps slowed. She looked at Fletch again. 'But you didn't have a hangover, did you? You weren't drunk. You were hypoglycaemic.'

'I *had* been in a taxi,' he said quietly. 'Someone saw the taxi driver stop and leave me at the side of the road. I'd been vomiting and I expect he made the same assumption you did.' Fletch's expression gave nothing away. 'Luckily that same person called the police who called an ambulance. I was having a seizure by the time they arrived. I spent a week in Intensive Care before I came out of the coma I went into.'

'What?' Kelly stopped in her tracks but Fletch kept walking. He went up the steps into the ambulance and Kelly saw him bend towards Ross and start talking.

Why had Fletch been in the intensive care unit? In a coma? How sick had he been, and why the hell hadn't she known anything about it?

She knew the answer to at least one of those questions. She hadn't known because she'd never tried to find out. She had made her assumptions and then her decisions and had acted on those decisions before allowing any time or influences that might change her mind.

And she had been wrong. Terribly wrong. The horror of that discovery made everything else pale into insignificance for the space of several heartbeats as Kelly watched the doors of the ambulance swing shut and cut off her view of Fletch.

She had thrown away her dreams. Her future with the only man that she had ever truly loved. And the choice had been based on a terrible mistake.

But it wasn't the end of the world, was it? Sometimes mistakes could be fixed. Fletch would understand once he knew why she'd had no choice but to make those decisions. There might even be some way to put things right.

There *had* to be a way.

CHAPTER SEVEN

REPERCUSSIONS from the disaster took on lives of their own.

Nobody could forget the impact the incident had had on so many people as the clean-up operation of Westgate Mall got into full swing during the following week. Coverage still dominated the media. TV cameras were present at every associated funeral. Newspapers followed the start of official inquiries into how the disaster had occurred. It was difficult to come to terms with the fact that the explosion had been a deliberate act of sabotage but blame was also being laid at the feet of a property development company and the City Council. The size of the blast might not have had such a devastating impact if building codes had been tighter and more strictly enforced.

Magazines and newspapers began to pick up human-interest stories from the lucky survivors and the families of those who had not been so lucky. The condition and progress of the seriously injured was being updated at frequent intervals. Lisa McCloud had been one of the unlucky ones. Kelly hoped that she had not regained consciousness enough to learn the fate of her precious daughters and her heart went out to Lisa's husband, who had lost his entire family.

Those who had been injured or affected whilst involved in the operations of the rescue services attracted the attention of the media and the sympathy of the public more than any others. Joe Barrington was a hero. He had risked his own life to save a five-year-old child. That the child was the son of another rescuer whose own mother had been killed in the incident was a bonus. The front-page picture in Wednesday morning's newspaper of Joe with Ricky in his arms and the accompanying account of the race through the rain of debris, the search for a frightened child and the long hours sheltering together in the back of a furniture truck made gripping reading. It also caused some amusement at ambulance headquarters. Kelly was back at work the day the article was published.

'Gorgeous photo, Joe,' she told him. 'I think you've been having us all on about hating kids.'

'No, he hasn't.' Kelly's crew partner, Callum Jones, was grinning. 'You've never worked with Joe, Kelly. You have no idea of the grumbling that comes with any job involving rug rats.'

Joe's expression gave nothing away. 'Ricky's all right...for a kid. At least he's quiet.'

'Says here he's autistic.'

'No wonder you managed to survive all that time shut in a van with him,' someone else quipped. 'You had a lot in common.'

'*Can* he talk?' Kelly asked. 'Jessica never said very much about his problems.'

'He can talk.' Joe sounded casual. He walked towards the kitchen area to make coffee. 'When he wants to.'

'His mother's a bit of all right.' Callum had turned to page three where there was a photograph of Jessica, her mother and a slightly younger Ricky.

'How is Jessica?' Kelly followed Joe away from the central table where crews were gathering ready to start the day shift. 'Did you see her last night? It was too late for me to get in after I'd been to visit Ross.'

'They're going to discharge Ricky today. Or maybe tomorrow. The swelling from his broken arm has gone down enough to change the cast and his other bruising is settling well.'

'I'm going down south with Jess tomorrow night. Her mother's funeral is on Friday. I've arranged a day off.'

'I know.' Joe smiled at Kelly. 'She told me. You're a good friend.'

'She'll need help. She's worried about how Ricky's going to cope.'

'She's not going to take him.'

'Really?' It was news to Kelly. 'But he's due to be discharged.'

'He's going to stay with me.' Joe seemed embarrassed by Kelly's surprise. 'Jessica's coming back after the funeral. There's a social worker at the hospital who's persuaded her to have Ricky assessed by a specialist educational service. He's going to go to school here for a couple of weeks.'

'Oh…' Kelly paused as the implications of this particular ripple surfaced. Then she smiled. Maybe something good might come out of this disaster after all. 'Good for you, Joe,' she said. 'Sounds like I'm not the only good friend Jessica's got.'

Joe shrugged off the praise. 'So how's Ross? I saw him just after the surgery yesterday. Sounds like it went pretty well.'

'They've stabilised the fracture dislocation at T10. The cervical fracture is stable enough to get away with a collar rather than traction. They won't know how good the result is going to be until after the spinal shock resolves, of course. It could take weeks.'

'He may get a good recovery.'

Kelly nodded. 'I doubt that he'll be running the Coast to Coast again, though.'

'Wendy must be devastated.'

'She is.' Kelly's quiet comment carried real empathy. Wendy and Ross had had so much in common with their love of physical pursuits.

And they had been so obviously deeply in love with each other. Was there any way their relationship could survive? It was more likely that this crisis had occurred too early and the fledgling love would be crushed under the strain. Kelly's heart went out to Wendy. She knew what it was like to be that much in love and to be faced with something that destroyed the kind of dreams for the future that all lovers cherished.

Kelly had been touched by the incident at a very personal level herself but there was no one with whom she could share the impact that Fletch's revelation had had. Her mother had too much to deal with right now. So had Wendy and Jessica. The more she thought about it over the next week, the worse it all seemed, however, and the more questions formed that Kelly wanted answers to. If Fletch had diabetes that was unstable enough to have caused such a major crisis, how could she not have noticed anything about it? It couldn't have been diagnosed that way. Or could it?

A run back to town, having transferred a patient to a rural hospital twenty minutes out of town, gave Kelly the chance to consult Callum. Well into his forties, Callum was a paramedic with many years' experience. He was also intelligent and interested in his career. Kelly was enjoying working with him.

'How much do you know about diabetes, Callum?'

'Heaps.' The response was less than modest. 'What do you want to know?'

'The diagnostic criteria are symptoms like thirst, weight loss, blurred vision and so on, plus a fasting glucose level greater than seven mils per litre, right?'

'Basically.'

'So diabetes is diagnosed when blood-glucose levels rise because of a lack of insulin production or interference with its function.'

'That's right.'

'Someone couldn't present with a hypogly-caemic crisis as the first symptom of diabetes, could they? They'd have to be already taking insulin for that to happen.' She and Fletch had spent so much time together—in bed and out of it. Surely she would have noticed him injecting himself? Or testing his blood-glucose level? Or seen the wealth of medical supplies he would have had to have available?

'If they're diabetic then the most common cause for a hypoglycaemic episode is an overdose of insulin or a missed meal or increased exercise. Or maybe an infection or too much alcohol.'

'Mmm.' Kelly tried not to get sidetracked by the mention of alcohol.

'Of course, there are other ways of becoming hypoglycaemic. You don't have to be diabetic.'

'No. Some drugs can do it,' Kelly agreed. 'Aspirin and beta-blockers.'

'Alcoholics or even binge drinkers are prone to it. Their livers don't have good stores of glycogen and missing a meal or two can precipitate a big fall in BGL.'

Back to alcohol again. Kelly knew that she had made a mistake making that assumption. No. There was a key to the puzzle that was missing here.

'There's carcinomas, too, of course.'

'Cancer!' Kelly was horrified. 'How could I have forgotten that? An insulin-secreting tumour could cause a major hypoglycaemic crisis.'

'I wouldn't beat yourself up over it.' Callum grinned. 'They're as rare as hen's teeth. Even if you work till you're seventy you'll probably never come across anyone who has one.'

Maybe she already had. Kelly was only half listening to the radio message that came through. She pulled out the map to check directions as Callum slowed and pulled the ambulance into a U-turn. She tried to keep her mind on the navigating but it wasn't easy.

'Go left at the next roundabout,' she instructed Callum. 'Do you know heaps about insulinomas as well?'

'Not really,' Callum admitted. 'They're islet cell tumours in the pancreas.'

Kelly swallowed. Is that what Fletch was living through now? A terminal illness? 'Would they treat themselves with glucagon?'

'Doubt it.' Callum was slowing again as he looked at street numbers. 'They'd use medication to suppress insulin secretion and probably IV infusions of glucose if things got out of control. I seem to remember that glucagon is contra-indicated.'

'Are they ever curable?'

'Sure. Only ten per cent are malignant and if it's just a single tumour it can be removed or part of the pancreas can be taken out. The overall cure rate is great.'

'Is it?' Kelly suddenly felt a lot happier. But, then, if Fletch had been cured, why would he still need to use something like glucagon? She intended to find out. She also intended to apologise. How or when she could tackle an apology that big was something that was proving progressively problematic, however.

The 'sick person' they had been diverted to attend to was a fifty-six-year-old man who had been unable to get out of bed that morning.

'Jim thinks he's had a stroke,' his wife informed the ambulance crew wearily as she led them into the house. 'He's had one before. I reckon he's just got a hangover and doesn't feel like going to work. He's done that more than once as well.'

It was Kelly's turn to do the assessment.

'Have I had another stroke?' The man's speech was slightly slurred.

Kelly could smell the alcohol. She could also smell the contents of the plastic container by the bed. 'Apart from the vomiting, Jim, what's been happening to you?'

'I can't get up. I can't talk properly. I feel really sick.'

Kelly turned to Jim's wife. 'Does his speech normally sound like this?'

'Only when he's been drinking.' The woman looked thoroughly fed up and Kelly could sympathise. She would make this assessment as brief and professional as possible. She noted that Jim's radial pulses were strong and equal on both sides. He looked pale and his skin was clammy.

'Let's get some vital signs, a BP and an ECG,' she instructed Callum. 'Jim, have you got any medical conditions you're being treated for?'

'High blood pressure.' His wife answered for him. 'And indigestion. And headaches. He's been getting a lot more of those lately.'

It all fitted with the clinical picture of a stroke presentation. 'Do you know what day it is today, Jim?' Kelly wanted to check her patient's level of consciousness.

'Wednesday.'

'And the date?'

'Sixteenth.'

'And you had a bit to drink last night?'

'Not that much.'

'BP's 190 over 105,' Callum reported. 'He's in sinus rhythm at a rate of 96.'

'Squeeze my hand,' Kelly ordered her patient. 'And this one.'

The hand grip was noticeably weaker on the right side. Kelly checked his feet to find the right-sided weakness still obvious. 'Smile at me, Jim. Show me all your teeth.'

The droop on the right side of the face added another piece to the picture.

'Have I had a stroke?'

'It looks like you may have.' Kelly nodded. 'We're going to take you into hospital so they can check you out properly.' She turned to Callum. 'I think nasal cannula will be enough for oxygen. I'll get an IV in and then we'll hit the road.'

She checked her patient again as they travelled to the hospital. Jim reported a pain score of six out of ten for the headache he still had.

'You didn't have a fall last night, did you?'

'Don't think so.'

Kelly examined his head for any sign of trauma. She listened to his chest and reassessed all the neurological signs and symptoms before documenting all the findings with care. Fletch might be on duty in Emergency again today and Kelly wanted her paperwork to be perfect. Under the provisional diagnosis slot she wrote 'CVA'. On arrival, the discovery that Neil Fletcher was on duty and was probably within earshot of the triage nurse made Kelly pay particular attention to her handover.

'Mr Wallace is fifty-six,' she stated. 'He has a previous history of hypertension and CVA. He woke with a severe headache, vomiting and right-sided paresis. No history of trauma. Strength is markedly diminished and he is unable to lift his right leg. Peripheral pulses are equal. GCS is 15. Pupils equal and reactive to light. Chest and abdomen are clear.' Kelly lowered her voice so that her patient couldn't overhear. 'He's vomited twice *en route* and there's still a strong odour of alcohol. Apparently his general consumption is pretty heavy.'

'Resus 3, thanks, Kelly.' The triage nurse put the paperwork on top of the central island bench, close to where Fletch was standing as he completed a phone call.

'What was the BGL?'

Busy manoeuvring the stretcher between the ECG and IV trolleys, it was easy for Kelly to pretend she hadn't heard the consultant's query. Callum looked apologetic.

'Sorry, Fletch. I didn't get that done.'

Kelly concentrated on where she was heading. She had been running that job. And she should have done a blood-glucose level. During the time it took to clean up the ambulance and ready themselves for a new call, Kelly became increasingly annoyed with herself. It was a basic vital sign measurement that should have been done. The distraction of a priority-one call to an accident on a building site was welcome.

The rest of the shift turned out to be busy enough to make it difficult for Kelly to follow up their CVA case. The opportunity came when Callum took advantage of their shift being due to finish to have a quick coffee with a mate in the ED staffroom.

'Really interesting case,' the triage nurse told Kelly. 'Turned out it wasn't a CVA at all.'

'What was it?'

'Hypoglycaemia. BGL was too low to record. We gave him some IV dextrose and the right-sided weakness and slurred speech disappeared in less than five minutes.'

'You're kidding.' Kelly shook her head. 'I've never seen a hypo present like that.'

'Neither had we.' The nurse grinned. 'Wish we could cure all our CVAs that easily.'

Kelly returned the smile with difficulty. Fletch would probably be wondering just how qualified she was to do her job right now. It had seemed like such a straightforward case of stroke. Coupled with the alcohol consumption, it had been enough for her to feel quite confident of the diagnosis. Had there been any suggestion of a lowered level of consciousness she would have checked the BGL automatically. The error was going to make it even harder to speak to Fletch but the background guilt Kelly was dealing with was enough to prompt her to walk past his office. Maybe she could throw in an apology for missing that diagnosis as well. It was small fry compared to the real apology she needed to make.

'Hi, Fletch.' Kelly poked her head around the door. 'Are you busy?'

'Not particularly.' Fletch didn't look welcoming but Kelly entered the office anyway. 'What can I do for you?'

'I…um…' Kelly took a very deep breath. There was no easy way to lead into this so she may as well get it over with. 'I wanted to apologise.'

'What for?'

'For thinking that…' Kelly hesitated and then tried again. 'When I left the country I had absolutely no idea that you were sick, Fletch.'

'Yes, you did.' The contradiction was matter-of-fact. 'You spoke to my flatmate. He told you I was sick and you said, ''I'm not surprised.'''

Kelly flushed. 'I thought he meant you had a hangover.'

'And that was enough for you to tell him to pass on the message that you never wanted to see me or speak to me again.'

'I… It was…' Kelly was completely at a loss now. She had known this would be difficult but what she hadn't factored in had been Fletch's response. Her mental preparation had seen him listening with increasing sympathy to a frank account of the kind of violence and emotional trauma she had grown up with thanks to her father's problem with alcohol. The worst-case scenario had been that he would refuse to speak to her or dismiss any apology. She hadn't expected an angry attack because she knew it wasn't justified. Not entirely.

'I was angry,' she said quietly. 'You put me in a position I couldn't handle.'

'And how did I do that?'

'That night in the restaurant.' Kelly avoided meeting Fletch's angry stare. 'It was…' She hesitated again. 'Really awful,' she finished in-adequately.

'It must have been.' The agreement was calm. 'I'd like to know what happened. Why don't you sit down and tell me about it, Kelly?'

It was a second opportunity that Kelly couldn't afford to pass up. She sat down slowly, trying to collect her thoughts. Unpleasant memories flooded back as soon as she started speaking.

'I had been really looking forward to going out that night. The meal was really nice and then it all started to go horribly wrong when I was having coffee and you were finishing that bottle of champagne. We were talking about having children.' Kelly swallowed painfully. 'We agreed that neither of us liked being only children and you thought we should start a family straight away so we could have three or four. I wanted to wait until I'd finished my paramedic qualification.'

'And?' Fletch's prompt was impatient. It all sounded perfectly reasonable to him so far, however troubling it was to have no memory of the conversation.

'You said the reason you were an only child was because your mother had left it too late to start a family. You started asking other people in the restaurant what they thought. You got very loud and you just wouldn't stop. You called the wine waiter over and asked his opinion. And then you ordered more champagne and they refused to give it to you.'

Kelly could almost feel the escalating embarrassment all over again. 'You decided to go to the toilet and you couldn't keep your balance when you tried to walk. You bumped into a waitress who dropped the plates she was carrying and a woman's dinner went all over her dress. We were asked to leave. We were asked to cover the cost of replacing the ruined meal. You refused. They threatened to call the police. You threw up on the floor in the middle of the restaurant.'

Fletch's eyes widened as he listened silently.

'Everybody thought you were drunk. Including me.' Especially me, Kelly added silently. 'I'd seen more than I wanted of behaviour like that in my life, which is the reason I don't drink alcohol myself.' Kelly gave her head a tiny shake. She didn't want to dredge up her family history quite yet. She had spent too many years keeping it hidden and Fletch was in no mood to listen sympathetically.

'I called a taxi for you,' she concluded calmly. 'And I stayed behind to try and sort things out. I paid for our meals, the meals that got dropped, the drycleaning for the woman's dress and the cost of having the carpet cleaned. People were walking out of the restaurant and the manager was threatening to sue us for lost business. I had never been so humiliated in my life.'

There was a long, long silence in the small office.

'I had no idea,' Kelly whispered finally, 'that it might have had a medical cause. I would never have sent you off in a taxi by yourself if I had. And I would never have considered breaking our engagement as a result.' She looked up and held Fletch's gaze. 'I made a dreadful mistake, Fletch, and I'm sorry. I'm terribly sorry.'

Fletch raised his eyebrows but his expression remained still. 'You thought I was obnoxiously drunk,' he said. 'And that was a good enough reason to dump me?'

'I thought you had a problem with alcohol,' Kelly amended. 'That you might be an alcoholic. It wasn't something I could deal with because—'

'You thought I was drunk,' Fletch interrupted. 'And that was enough to leave a message that you'd pass on marrying me, thanks.' He shook his head. 'You never really loved me at all, did you, Kelly?'

'That's not true! I—'

'Even if I *had* been paralytically intoxicated on that one occasion, it shouldn't have made any difference. Not if there'd been any genuine love on your part.'

'It was because it *was* genuine that it made such a difference. I wanted to spend the rest of my life with you, Fletch.' Kelly was desperate to make him understand. 'It was knowing that I might be making the same mistake my mother did that made me realise I couldn't do it.'

Fletch wasn't listening any longer. Not properly. He wasn't looking angry now either. He was looking disgusted. 'You always did have a holier than thou attitude to drinking. Just because you choose not to touch the stuff, it doesn't mean that's what everybody should do. People can drink alcohol sensibly and enjoy it. They can even be forgiven for having too much on the odd occasion. But not by you, obviously. That's sheer arrogance, Kelly Drummond. You make assumptions all the time, don't you? And you're so sure you're right.'

'I don't,' Kelly protested.

'And what about this morning? That patient of yours was terrified he'd had another stroke and would be paralysed for life this time. You'd made up your mind and that was that.'

'It was a classic presentation of a CVA.'

'And let's face it, you'd already decided that he had a problem with alcohol and you wanted to get the job over and done with.'

Kelly didn't want to admit the element of truth in the statement, even to herself. 'I know

I should have done a BGL. That was a mistake.'

'You make a lot of mistakes, don't you, Kelly?'

Kelly stood up. It was time to leave. It had been a certainly been a mistake thinking she could apologise to Fletch. He wasn't interested. The damage was irreparable. She barely acknowledged the thanks given to her by the relatives of the last patient she had brought in as she walked back through the emergency department. She bypassed the staffroom in favour of waiting for Callum out in the ambulance. How long would it be before the people she had to work with here gleaned the attitude of the consultant who knew her better than anyone else in this department? Fletch thought she was cold-hearted and ruthless. Selfish. Now she could add arrogant and probably professionally incompetent to the list.

Neil Fletcher hated her.

Kelly sighed heavily. It was easy enough to see things from his point of view. He had no memory of their last evening together and no inkling that any reminder of the kind of humiliation Kelly had grown up with would be enough to make her panic. He had simply been dumped without explanation and at a time when he would have been more in need of support than he'd ever been. He must have really loved her to still feel so angry after all this time.

Kelly buried her face in her hands. She hoped Callum would take his time over his coffee. She wasn't in any hurry to go home. She had never expected her break-up with Fletch to come back to haunt her so directly. Or that it would become so interwoven with the problems that faced her at home. There was no escape from Fletch, whatever direction she took.

Fletch was right. She had made a lot of mistakes. And one of them had been returning to New Zealand. She couldn't change the past and she couldn't escape it. She had allowed it to destroy her future.

And she still had the present to deal with.

CHAPTER EIGHT

SHE hadn't made any mistakes this time.

The patient was intubated. Kelly was close to the head of the stretcher, moving with it, squeezing the ventilation bag with practised regularity as she handed the patient over to the waiting emergency trauma team.

'His name is John Woodbury. He's twenty-five years old. He was the driver in a high-speed, head-on car v. car.'

They were through the doors of the resus room now. Kelly pushed an IV stand out of her way. 'GCS was 9 on arrival. Breathing deteriorated rapidly due to a tension pneumothorax.'

Fletch could see the chest decompression cannula taped into place. The oxygen saturation recording was sitting at a perfectly acceptable ninety-five per cent now so the procedure had clearly been successful.

'He's been intubated with a size 7 tube without complications. Cardiac function was also compromised with a period of VT that resolved spontaneously on decompression.'

Staff had positioned themselves to move the patient to the trauma bed.

'On your count, Kelly.' Fletch reached for a handle of the backboard.

'On three,' Kelly instructed. 'One, two... three.'

The young man was now on the bed. A nurse began cutting away remnants of clothing. Another was hanging up two bags of saline.

'He's got two 14-gauge cannulae *in situ*,' Kelly informed Fletch. 'Both patent. He's had three litres of saline so far.'

'What was the blood pressure on arrival?'

'Eighty over 40.'

It was now 95 over 60. The fluid replacement had also been a potentially life-saving procedure. Now Fletch had to direct his team to finding the source of internal haemorrhage and stopping it.

'There's no sign of any obvious cervical or head injury. Trachea was midline.'

Fletch nodded. The collar was now preventing his own assessment of the cervical spine and neck but he trusted Kelly's judgement.

'He has multiple left-sided rib fractures and subcutaneous emphysema. There's also left-sided abdominal distension.'

Probably a ruptured spleen. As long as the control of the patient's airway and respiration was secure, they could get this young man up to Theatre quickly. Thanks to Kelly's management they did not need to take any extra time to intubate and gain venous access.

'He has bilateral open fractures of his tib and fib.' A nurse lifted the dressings on both John's legs and Fletch nodded grimly.

'Give Orthopaedics a call. And get a surgical registrar down here, stat. We'll do a log roll and check his back and then I want X-rays of the C-spine, chest and pelvis. Type and cross-match for blood.' Fletch continued his list of instructions as Kelly and her crew partner began to collect their gear. The portable oxygen cylinder and cardiac monitor were put on top of the bloodstained sheet covering the stretcher. Kelly positioned herself to help with the log roll and then she slid the backboard clear of the bed. Callum took it into the adjacent decontamination shower room. Kelly pushed the stretcher clear of the working area around the bed and then moved to a corner behind the nurse documenting the resuscitation. She clearly had not had a chance to complete any of her own paperwork *en route*.

Fletch found himself watching Kelly as he moved behind the shield when the overhead X-ray equipment came into use. He should tell her what a good job she had done here but he had barely spoken to her since the aftermath of that case of hypoglycaemia and he recognised how unfair it had been to accuse her of any incompetency over that patient. It had been a classic stroke presentation and it wasn't as if the oversight hadn't been picked up and corrected before any lasting damage had occurred.

Everybody made mistakes. Fletch had made a few of his own over the years. He turned his

gaze deliberately away from the sight of
Kelly's bent head with the long, dark plait
hanging over one shoulder and the look of concentration on those well-remembered features.
Fletch's mistakes had been more concerned
with women than patient management and he
wasn't stupid enough to make the same mistake twice. He had been reminding himself of
that for the last three weeks.

So what if Kelly hadn't dumped him because he'd been sick? That she'd never come
to see him in hospital because she'd had no
knowledge of his admission? It made no difference. In fact, maybe it made things worse.
She had broken their engagement on the
strength of one bad night out and on the assumption that he'd lost control because he'd
had too much to drink. To be prepared to break
off what was supposed to be the most significant relationship in her life and to cut off any
contact without explanation was a pretty
damning indication that the available love
would never have lasted into marriage. He was
lucky to have escaped. Stray thoughts that
Kelly might have had some justification for her

actions had been occurring to Fletch with disturbing frequency since that session in his office but her story wasn't enough to convince him.

Or was it?

Callum emerged from the shower room with the clean backboard and Kelly smiled her thanks just as the X-rays were completed and Fletch moved back to his patient. He had seen that smile so often in the past. A recognition for even the smallest act of caring—a cup of coffee maybe, or a word of encouragement. It had always made the service worthwhile. Made Fletch want to do more to show how much he cared.

'That was a good job, Kelly.' Fletch's tone was more brusque than he had intended. Surely he didn't feel jealous that it was Callum who had received that smile? 'Well done.'

'Thanks.' Kelly's smile had begun to fade the instant Fletch had spoken. The fact that she didn't even make eye contact was a put-down. Fletch moved past briskly. He had been right all along. Her story made no difference and he wasn't going to set himself up to get slapped down by this woman again.

So why did he continue to notice her every time she came into the department? It wasn't as if he was directly involved in the care of any of her patients over the next week or so, yet he could virtually list them—an old lady with a fractured hip, a toddler with an epileptic seizure, chest pains and heart attacks, abdominal pains and an amputated finger.

Then there was the case of hypoglycaemia that Kelly had treated with IV glucose but transported to hospital because she'd been unhappy with the response. He eavesdropped on that particular handover.

'Mrs Seule is an insulin-dependent diabetic who's having trouble controlling her BGL. This is the third episode of hypoglycaemia she's experienced this week despite lowering her insulin dose. Her husband tried to get her to take oral glucose but she vomited and was unresponsive on our arrival.'

Fletch tended to vomit when his BGL dropped low enough. That was why he used glucagon when he knew his symptoms were becoming critical. Not that he used it often. Most of the time he was perfectly normal— just as he had been when he knew Kelly. No wonder she'd been so shocked when he'd told her he was diabetic. And no wonder she'd been puzzled. Strictly speaking, he wasn't diabetic. He'd only needed IV dextrose treatment once in the last year and his insulin levels very rarely created any problems at all.

Kelly finished her handover and was about to transfer her patient to a bed. The woman reached up and took the paramedic's hand.

'Thank you so much, my dear. You've been so kind. Don gets so worried when I have one of my little turns.'

Fletch wondered if Mrs Seule had any clear idea of what her behaviour was like during a hypoglycaemic episode. He doubted that she became combative or unpleasant. Mr Seule was beside his wife, holding her hand. He added his thanks and won a smile from Kelly.

'You're very welcome.' The words were sincere. And warm.

Fletch knew perfectly well that Kelly wasn't cold-hearted or ruthless. He had been unfair and he didn't like the prickles of guilt that continued to make their presence felt as one busy day followed another. He knew what Kelly's real character was like. She was determined. And courageous. She would go through whatever she had to in order to achieve what she knew had to be done, but she wouldn't do it unless she'd weighed up the pros and cons. For whatever reason, Kelly had believed she had been justified in taking the action she had against Fletch and that explained why she had considered an apology from him appropriate.

Was there any justification? Just how obnoxious had he been that night at the restaurant? Had he been more than argumentative and uncoordinated? Fletch tried to concentrate on the X-ray in front of him but he wasn't calculating the degree of pulmonary oedema his patient had with any degree of accuracy. It had been unpleasant but dismissible to have a period of time, however brief, of which he had absolutely no memory. It was a lot less easy to dismiss now that he knew he had behaved so appallingly. And so completely out of character. It sounded as though he'd been a loudmouthed hoon with no regard at all for public decency.

It was hardly surprising that Kelly might have been shocked into second thoughts about the man she'd been planning to marry. It wasn't as though they had really known each other that well. It had been a whirlwind romance with the engagement coming little more than two months after their first date. Fletch had never felt, and never could feel, that strongly about any other woman. And he had been so sure that Kelly had felt the same way. Maybe she had. And maybe he had been abusive enough that night to scare her into running. Maybe she had waited for an apology and reassurance that had never come. Kelly had admitted she'd made a mistake. *She* had apologised.

Did she deserve another chance? Fletch pulled the X-ray from the viewing screen with a decisive snap as he turned to scan the department for Kelly's whereabouts. Perhaps he could arrange some time they could spend together. A coffee or a meal. Enough time to explore the possibility that there might still be a spark somewhere amongst the embers of their relationship. But what Fletch saw were the taillights of the ambulance as it pulled away from the loading bay. Kelly had gone.

Fletch strode towards Resus 4 where his patient in heart failure awaited his opinion. It was just as well Kelly had left the department. The moment of personal indecision would pass swiftly, just like the flashes of attraction that he'd been experiencing ever since she'd stepped back into his professional orbit. His body might still have memories of his overwhelming attraction to Kelly, and it was possible that his heart still had the capacity for emotional involvement, but his brain had matured a lot in the last couple of years. It was more than capable of counteracting and overriding any signals that might make reawakening even a friendship with Kelly Drummond seem like a good idea.

Reawakening friendships was not always a good idea. Kelly stood a little to one side of the group of people gathered at a local winery on this warm spring evening. She sipped her orange juice with little enjoyment. Why had it seemed like a good idea to accept the invitation when Dave Stewart had rung last week? She had known Fletch would probably attend this reunion of their USAR course class. She had even convinced herself that it would be good to see him socially. It was becoming routine for them to avoid each other when they met professionally. Almost easy, in fact. If she could handle the distance in a social setting, maybe it would provide some kind of closure. She could accept that she had ruined her chance with Fletch, put a stop to any forlorn hopes of putting things right and move on.

There were plenty of people here that Kelly had been looking forward to seeing. It had been too simple to focus on the situation at home and withdraw from involvement anywhere else outside work. The busier she had kept herself, the better able she had been to feel optimistic about getting through this particular patch of her life, but regrets about how out of touch she had become were now undermining that optimism. Kelly moved towards Wendy who had just broken away from a conversation with Joe.

'I'm sorry I haven't been out to visit Ross for a while.'

'That's OK. He knows how busy you are.'

'It's the height of the season for the daffodils. When I'm not at work I'm helping my mother get the blooms picked and packed for the market. She can't afford to hire extra help at the moment.' Kelly knew her excuse was lame. Her mother had coped alone with the small flower farm while she had been in Australia. 'How are things going at the moment?'

'Not great. I wanted Ross to come tonight. He's quite independent in his wheelchair now and getting out for the first time would have been a major hurdle to get through, but he refused to even discuss it.'

'I guess being out with us might be too much of a reminder of the accident and everything he's lost.'

'It's been nearly two months. He's got to face up to it some time.' Wendy looked tired and sounded uncharacteristically dispirited.

'We all have to accept things that can't be changed and move on.'

Kelly nodded with heartfelt agreement. That was precisely what she was doing, wasn't it? She could see Fletch talking to Roger and Owen and she wasn't experiencing any overwhelming feelings of loss. Or even attraction. If anything, Kelly just felt a little sad. Maybe Wendy's mood was contagious. She looked away from Fletch.

'How's Jessica, do you know? She still sounded pretty upset when I spoke to her last week.' Kelly's gaze was searching the gathering. 'Joe hasn't said anything much about the break-up. In fact, I hardly seem to see him around headquarters these days.'

'She's gone back to her old job. She told me she's determined to pick up the pieces and get on with her life.'

'Good for her.' Kelly was looking at Joe now. It was simply a coincidence that he happened to be standing next to Fletch. 'Such a shame, though. I really thought those two were made for each other.'

'Like me and Ross?' Wendy murmured. She looked ready to cry.

'You and Ross are going to be fine. You'll get through this.' Kelly's gaze was still caught by Joe and Fletch. They both had tall glasses of beer in their hands and Kelly was suddenly conscious of the drink she was holding. She was sick to death of drinking orange juice. No wonder it came across as a holier than thou attitude about alcohol. She eyed the glass in Wendy's hand.

'I think I'd like a glass of wine.'

Wendy finished her drink and smiled. 'You're right, Kelly. I'm not about to give up on Ross. Let's both find a glass of wine and drink to the future. Preferably on the other side of this vineyard. I'm getting really fed up with the way Kyle keeps staring at me.'

Wendy's planned escape didn't quite eventuate. The two women had to pause when Dave wanted an update on Ross. They were joined by Owen and Roger and then Kyle managed to tag onto the amalgamation that saw Fletch and Joe join the conversation. Kelly stepped back a little as a waiter came past bearing a tray of wine. She swapped her orange juice for one of the long-stemmed glasses. Pleasantly surprised by the taste of the sparkling white wine, Kelly took several sips before tuning back in to the conversation around her.

'It *was* a trial by fire, wasn't it?'

'Let's hope you don't lay on the kind of practical follow-up we had for your next USAR course.'

'You guys are the best trained team we've got now.' Dave sounded proud of the class.

'I keep my kit packed. It sits right beside my bedroom door.' Kyle was as enthusiastic as ever. 'I'm ready for the next call-out. How 'bout you, Wendy?'

'I can't say I've thought about it.' Wendy edged sideways to get further away from Kyle. 'It's not something that's very likely to happen, is it?'

'You never know.' Joe seemed as subdued as Wendy was. 'We thought that before the last call-out, I seem to remember.'

'Have they got any closer to finding out who planted that bomb?'

'They're not likely to, in my opinion.' Kyle sounded knowledgeable enough to make Wendy roll her eyes at Kelly. The almost imperceptible jerk of her head was a plea for escape. Kyle was still speaking as they slipped away from the group. 'I heard that the video surveillance tapes were destroyed—and anyway, how could they trace someone who could have left a bomb programmed to go off days later?'

'This wine is nice,' Kelly told Wendy.

'I'll have another one,' Wendy decided. 'And then I'm going home. I don't really feel like being sociable. Especially with Kyle being here. Do you know, I don't think he feels any responsibility over Ross's accident at all? If he hadn't been stupid enough to get that spike through his leg it would never have happened.'

'The injury wasn't serious enough to slow him down much, was it?' Kelly glanced over her shoulder. Kyle was still standing near Fletch. 'I don't really feel like being sociable either. I think another wine is an excellent idea.'

The general consensus a short time later that the group should move on to a nightclub gave Wendy the excuse to leave. Kelly intended to do likewise.

'I need to go home,' she told Joe. 'It's getting late.'

'Oh, come on.' Joe put his arm around Kelly. 'It might cheer you up.' He peered at his colleague more closely. 'You look about as bad as I feel. What's up?'

Kelly almost laughed. Where should she start? With the fact that her father had been released from prison a few days ago and her mother was too nervous to answer the phone? With the offer of her old job in Melbourne, an option Kelly was very tempted to consider? With the knowledge that, however hard she tried to move on, she would never quite come to terms with the low opinion Fletch now had of her?

'Do you know,' she said seriously to Joe, 'that some people think I'm shellfise?'

'Sorry?' Joe looked confused.

Kelly concentrated on her enunciation. 'I meant selfish.' Heavens, nobody got drunk on two glasses of bubbly wine, did they? 'Selfish *and* cold-hearted,' Kelly expanded. She felt ridiculously close to tears. 'Some people really hate me.'

'Oh, rot!' Joe was grinning now. 'Stay here. I'm going to see if there's a taxi left that we can fit into.'

Kelly saw Joe have a quick word to Fletch as he walked towards the car park. She saw Fletch frown as he looked in her direction. And then he started moving. Kelly looked around quickly. Everybody was leaving and she didn't want to be left alone with Fletch. The courtyard bar was flanked by rows of grapevines. Kelly ducked behind the leafy cover. She would have got a lot further if her legs hadn't felt so wobbly. The hand supporting her elbow really wasn't necessary, however.

'Let go,' Kelly instructed Fletch. 'I'm going home now.'

'Really?' Fletch looked faintly amused. 'You weren't planning to drive, were you?'

'Yesh.' Then Kelly frowned. She couldn't go home. Not yet. Quite apart from it being extremely inadvisable for her to attempt driving, she probably reeked of alcohol and what would her mother say if she knew Kelly had been drinking? Why *had* she been drinking? And why was Fletch holding her arm like this? Not that it wasn't rather nice. Kelly smiled up at her companion.

'I don't really want to go home,' she confided.

'Where do you want to go?' Fletch's look of amusement had been replaced by something like curiosity. Or possibly astonishment.

'With you,' Kelly said firmly. She leaned closer to Fletch, resting her head on his arm. 'I've missed you so much, Fletch.' The soft hiccup didn't detract from the sincerity of her statement. 'I still love you, you know.'

'*What?*' Fletch's expression had gone past astonishment. He looked appalled.

'I love you.' Kelly hadn't realised the truth until the words had passed her lips. Having said them and recognised how true they were, her feelings for Fletch became overwhelming. 'I really, really love you, Fletch.' She put her arms around his neck and pulled his head towards her as she stood on tiptoe.

And then she kissed him.

Fletch *was* appalled but it all happened far too fast for him to do anything about it. And then, suddenly, he didn't *want* to do anything about it. The sensation of Kelly's lips on his, the smell of her hair and the scent of her skin filling his nostrils...the taste of her mouth. He had forgotten none of it and it was all just as sweet as it always had been. Time stood still. Moved backwards, in fact, because for a few seconds Fletch completely forgot the pain and anger he had associated with memories of exactly this kind of physical contact. His hands moved of their own accord to rest above Kelly's hips, to slide up over her ribs, his thumbs grazing her breasts before he pulled her deeper into the kiss.

It was the sound Kelly made that broke the spell, a tiny mew halfway between a sign and a moan. The well-remembered sign that the kiss was not going to be nearly enough to satisfy her. Somehow the addition of the extra sense triggered an overload switch and Fletch knew precisely where he was and what was happening. What he didn't *want* to happen. He let go of Kelly's body and used his hands to disentangle her arms from around his neck. He pushed her away firmly enough to make her stagger slightly.

'I don't want this, Kelly.'

'You don't really hate me, do you, Fletch?' Dark blue eyes held an appeal that was difficult to resist. 'If you hadn't loved me, you wouldn't still be so angry with me.' The eyes filled with tears. 'I made a dreadful mistake, Fletch. And I'm sorry. I feel so...so...' Kelly paused and swallowed. She suddenly looked a lot paler than she had a minute ago. 'Sick,' she finished. 'Oh, hell, Fletch. I'm going to be *sick*!'

Fletch held her head as she leaned into the nearest available screen of grape leaves.

'Feel any better?' he enquired wryly a minute later.

Kelly looked terrible. She wiped the perspiration from her forehead and pushed damp curls behind her right ear. She didn't look at

Fletch. Or at Joe as he completed his search for her.

'I guess you don't feel like coming to the nightclub, then?'

'Sorry, Joe,' Kelly said faintly. 'I'm not feeling very well.'

Fletch winked at Joe. 'I think I'd better take Kelly home.'

She offered no protest this time. Kelly handed over her car keys and followed Fletch. She climbed into the front passenger seat of her car, leaned back and closed her eyes. 'I'm never, ever going to drink alcohol again.'

'Two glasses of wine in a short space of time when you've never touched the stuff before probably isn't a good idea,' Fletch agreed. 'At least you've got rid of most of it. You'll feel better very soon. Now—are you still living out in the sticks with your mother?'

'Yes.' Kelly felt too awful to try and think up anywhere else to go right now. It wasn't just the effects of the alcohol. She was mortified by her behaviour. She had dumped Fletch because she'd thought he'd been drunk when he hadn't been. Now she was drunk and he was looking after her. Fletch was right in that the effects of the remaining alcohol in her system were wearing off quickly, but she wasn't feeling any better. The more sober Kelly became the worse she felt.

What was worse—much worse—than the drinking was that she had told him how she felt. She had *kissed* him with all the passion she had unknowingly bottled up for so long. And he had rejected her. Pushed her away. Told her that he didn't want her.

It was a twenty-minute drive to the flower farm on the outskirts of Christchurch that Kelly and her mother had purchased together soon after her father's imprisonment. It had been a new start for both of them, with all the promise of a brighter future, and right now it was a haven that Kelly was looking forward to reaching. She kept her eyes firmly closed to discourage any conversation. She didn't want to talk to Fletch any more. After this, she never even wanted to see him again.

'Here we are.' The car tyres were crunching over the gravel driveway.

Kelly opened her eyes reluctantly as the vehicle stopped. She reached for the doorhandle. 'Thanks,' she muttered.

'Are you going to be all right now?' Fletch was peering towards the house. 'I don't think anyone's home. Unless your mother's gone to bed already.'

'Probably.' Kelly opened her door. 'It's pretty late, isn't it?'

'Nearly eleven.' Fletch was still staring at the house. 'Does your mother usually leave the front door open when she's gone to bed?'

'Of course not. I've got my own key.' Kelly was pleased to find she was thinking clearly again. Now all she needed was something for her headache and a good night's sleep and she could forget all about this whole horrible evening. She climbed out of the car and slammed the door behind her.

The sound had a fainter echo. It wasn't until Fletch was standing beside her that Kelly realised it had been the sound of his own door closing.

'I don't like this.'

'What?' For a wild second Kelly thought he meant that he didn't want them to part on such a bad note. That he had changed his mind about rejecting her. But Fletch wasn't looking at Kelly. He was staring ahead of them at the front door of the house.

Kelly stared, too. And blinked. Perhaps her brain wasn't as clear as she'd thought. It wasn't that the door was unlocked—it was standing open. An invitation to enter a totally unlit house. Kelly swallowed. She didn't like it either.

'Stay here,' Fletch ordered. 'I'm going to have a look inside.'

Kelly let him go ahead but only because it took a second or two to break the stunning effect that the implications of the open door generated. The hall light was on by the time Kelly ran up the steps to the verandah. The light in the sitting room that led from the hall-way at the front of the house was also on. Kelly stopped abruptly when she saw Fletch crouched in the middle of the room. A figure lay sprawled in front of him. Kelly could see that she was unconscious. She could also see some of the injuries that had been inflicted.

'Oh, my God!' she breathed. *'Mum!'*

Fletch glanced up swiftly at the sound of Kelly's voice. 'She's alive,' he said curtly. 'Call an ambulance, Kelly.'

CHAPTER NINE

NEIL FLETCHER'S leadership ability and professional skills had never been more welcome.

'Have you called the ambulance?'

'They're on their way. ETA twelve minutes.'

'Good girl. Have you got a kit available? A stethoscope and BP cuff?'

Kelly nodded. She was back only seconds later with the kit she carried in her car.

'Hold her head for me, Kelly. We can't rule out a C-spine injury.'

Kelly had to swallow a huge lump in her throat as she touched the matted, bloodstained hair on one side of her mother's head. Fletch removed a stethoscope and then a penlight from the kit. He listened to her chest then lifted Kath Drummond's eyelids one at a time and shone the bright beam onto her pupils.

'Her airway's clear at the moment but I don't like the bruising on her neck. I think she may be in for some pharyngeal oedema. Pupils are a bit sluggish but I couldn't find any obvious skull fracture.' Fletch glanced up at Kelly's white face. 'Talk to her, Kelly. She's not responsive but she may still be able to hear you.'

'Mum?' Kelly's voice cracked and she had to try again. 'It's OK, Mum. You're going to be all right. Fletch is taking care of you.'

Fletch was checking the bruised area on Kath's neck again. Then he felt the bones of her face. One eye was blackened and swelling rapidly—it would soon be impossible to check pupil reactivity on that side. A lip was split and had bled copiously. Kelly was also aware of the blood seeping between her fingers.

'I need a dressing, Fletch. She's still losing blood from this head wound.'

'Hmm.' Fletch's gaze wandered for a moment. 'It looks like she fell backwards and hit her head. There's blood on the corner of that coffee-table.'

Kelly fought off a wave of nausea as she watched Fletch rip open a package containing a large gauze pad. He folded the dressing and put his hand over Kelly's to keep their patient's head stable as he slipped the dressing over the wound. Then he pressed Kelly's hand down.

'Keep firm pressure on that.' The instruction was unnecessary but welcome nonetheless. So was the contact of Fletch's hand. Kelly caught his gaze and that gave her additional strength. Thank God he was here. She could handle this. Fletch would make sure of that.

'You realise she's been attacked?' Fletch asked quietly. 'It looks as though someone's tried to strangle her. We'll have to call the police.' There was a deeper question in Fletch's eyes. A question that was laced with concern. 'Have you got any idea why this might have happened? Or who might be responsible?'

Kelly bit her lip. She closed her eyes tightly as she hesitated for a second. Then she shook her head. She should tell him that she had a very good idea of who and why, but she couldn't. The shameful secret had been buried too long and Fletch hadn't expected any answers anyway.

Kelly kept hold of her mother's head and watched as Fletch finished his assessment. He checked for chest and abdominal injuries, listened to her breathing again, took her blood pressure and pulse and monitored her condition and level of consciousness. He kept Kelly informed as he went.

'Chest is clear and abdo's soft.

'BP's 110 on 70. Your mum's not normally hypertensive, is she? Is she on any kind of medication?'

Kelly shook her head. 'She's very healthy. She doesn't have any cardiac or respiratory conditions. She's not diabetic. She's never had a hospital admission.' Though she should have, Kelly added silently. The GP had dealt with injuries in the past that should have been seen in hospital. And sometimes even the GP hadn't seen them. Kelly took a deep breath. 'She was concussed once—a few years ago.'

Fletch's glance was sharp. 'How did that happen?'

What had the story been? 'She fell and hit her head on a kitchen cupboard.'

'Was she KO'd?'

'Very briefly.'

'Was she assessed in ED?'

'No. She refused to go near the hospital.' Kelly looked away from Fletch. 'I know, I know. I tried to persuade her. I kept a very close eye on her. I think she had headaches for a few weeks afterwards but there were no indications of any serious repercussions.'

Fletch rubbed his knuckle on her mother's collarbone. 'Kath? Can you hear me? Open your eyes, love.'

Kath groaned and tried to move her head.

'It's OK, Mum.' Kelly increased her grip on the sides of her mother's head. 'Don't try to move. We're looking after you. You're going to be all right.' She could hear the siren getting closer now. It was the first time Kelly had experienced the kind of relief that sound could produce. The equipment and expertise her mother needed was on its way.

Had she been given a choice, Kelly would have picked Callum Jones to be leading the ambulance crew but as they were on their rostered days off he was the last person she actually expected to see come through the door.

'Callum! What are you doing on the road?'

'Overtime.' Callum wasn't smiling. 'Control said this was your home address.' He was still looking at Kelly as he removed a high-concentration oxygen mask from the bag attached to the portable cylinder.

'It is,' Kelly confirmed. 'This is my mum, Kath.'

'What happened?'

Kelly paused just long enough for Fletch to give her a curious glance before speaking himself. 'She's been beaten up. She was unresponsive when we found her. Facial injuries, query fractured cheekbone, split lip, head injury and some nasty bruising on her neck. Looks like someone's had a go at strangling her.'

'Trachea's midline.' Callum was looking at the fingermarks on Kath's neck as he slipped the oxygen mask into place. He touched the swollen cheekbone gently and shook his head. 'Have the police been called?'

'Not yet.'

'It wasn't a sexual attack, was it?'

'Oh, God!' Kelly hadn't even thought of that. 'No…he wouldn't have done something like that.'

Both Callum and Fletch gave her a strange look. Callum looked away quickly. 'How long has she had that stridor?'

'It's been increasing over the last couple of minutes. Probably pharyngeal oedema. Maybe we should intubate now while we've got the opportunity.'

Callum nodded. 'Why don't you do that, Fletch? I'll get a line in and start some fluids.' He glanced at his crew partner. 'Mandy, get hold of the police and then bring a stretcher in. Grab a collar as well.'

There was nothing that Kelly needed to do other than provide stability and reassurance. She watched as the team around her efficiently did everything they needed to do to prepare their patient for transport. Fletch did not seem to consider relinquishing the care of Kath to the paramedics, and both he and Kelly remained with the crew as they travelled back to hospital. They passed a police car with its lights and siren on going in the opposite direction. The police would presumably examine and secure the scene at the house before arriving at the hospital to continue their enquiries.

Fletch took control of the trauma room team and Kelly stayed with her mother. Kath's breathing was stabilised, sedation and more pain relief administered, X-rays were taken and a CT scan arranged. Kelly provided the information needed on personal details and past medical history.

'Don't forget the previous head injury,' Fletch reminded her. 'That's significant.'

Fletch left the trauma room when he needed to talk to the neurosurgical registrar.

'I'll organise Theatre. We'll take her straight up after the CT. I'm pretty sure we're going to find a haematoma that needs draining. We don't want intracranial pressure rising any further.'

The loud banging on the outside door of the ambulance loading bay covered Fletch's affirmative reply. Both men looked towards the source of the sound. An ambulance crew was attempting to shift a middle-aged man away from the doors so that they could bring a stretcher in. Fletch could hear the shouting as the doors opened.

'You can't tell me to get lost. You can get stuffed, mate.' The words were slurred. 'I'm coming in to find her.'

He pushed past the ambulance officers, staggered and almost fell. The triage nurse was now aware of what was happening.

'Call Security,' she advised the booking clerk. *'Now!'*

The internal doors had opened automatically and the inebriated man gazed around the emergency department triumphantly.

'Where the hell is she?' he demanded loudly. 'I've got something I want to say to the interfering little bitch.'

Fletch was the closest person to the unwelcome intruder. 'Who is it that you're looking for?' If he could keep him talking for a minute or two, the security officers would have a chance to get here before anyone was threatened more than verbally.

'She's always been trouble.' The man peered at Fletch. 'Who the hell are you?'

'A doctor.'

'You don't look like a doctor.' Alcohol-laden fumes washed over Fletch as the man leaned towards him. Shorter and leaner than Fletch, unshaven and with bloodshot eyes, he didn't look like he would take too much strength to manage, but who knew whether he was concealing any weapons? The anger the man radiated was enough to make him much more dangerous than his size would suggest.

'Five years,' he informed Fletch with disgust. 'Five whole years without a bloody drink, and for what? So she can tell me to get stuffed. She's getting rid of me.' He spat on the floor. 'I know who told her to say that and she's going to pay. Big time.'

'What's your name?' Fletch could see two security officers advancing.

'None of your bloody business.' The touch of a security officer on his arm was enough to further enrage the man. He took a swing at Fletch and missed as the doctor ducked sideways. Then he aimed a fist at the security officer. He was stronger than he looked and the scuffle to control him took enough time and effort to create chaos. A trolley was upended.

A woman screamed. And the door to the trauma room opened.

For a split second, the sense of *déjà vu* was enough to negate any reality in the scene. Kelly's instinctive reaction was to protect her mother. She closed the door behind her and stood with her back against the large handle. The prod of metal against her spine was real enough. And so was what she was facing. Kelly's past had come to claim her. There was no escape.

There had never been any escape.

'Kelly…love.' The figure between the security officers stopped struggling. 'Tell them who I am.'

All eyes were on Kelly. The whole department was at a standstill. Kelly could sense the shock that there might be some connection between her and the violent drunk who had caused such an unpleasant disruption. And Fletch was there. Staring as hard as everyone else. Looking as shocked as everyone else.

'Get him out of here,' Kelly said calmly. 'Call the police.'

'You *bitch*!' The beseeching tone was gone instantaneously. The man's face twisted in rage and he wrenched an arm free from a guard. He managed one step towards Kelly. 'You can't do this to me. I'm your *father*!'

There was a deadly silence. Kelly felt sick. She shook her head to try and clear the odd ringing sound in her ears. She took a very shaky breath.

'You're not my father.' The words sounded remarkably clear. Almost loud in the continuing silence. 'You never were.' It was hard even looking at the man in front of her. The effort it took to maintain eye contact and control her fear enough to speak made the words sound forced and icily cold. 'And you're never going to hurt my mother again. The police will be here any minute now and this time they'll lock you away for good. I hope they throw away the key.'

Kelly wasn't sure what happened first after her words died away into the silence. Perhaps everything happened simultaneously. Her father broke free of both security officers. They lunged after him. Fletch also moved. His body was in front of Kelly, protecting her. Fletch lost his balance as a security guard fell against him and then his arms were around Kelly, spinning her to face the door and pressing her into the safety of his hold. Her senses were heightened by the rush of adrenaline. She could see nothing but she could smell the scent of Fletch's skin and could feel his warmth and strength. She could hear the shouting and the movement. She could even hear the swish of the automatic doors to the ambulance loading bay opening.

'You're safe now, Kelly. He's gone.'

The security officers had also gone. And then one appeared back at a run.

'We lost him,' he announced nervously. 'Where the hell are the police?'

Kelly pulled away from Fletch. She had to get back to her mother.

'Kelly?'

She met his gaze for only a fraction of a second. She didn't want to try and analyse what she saw in his eyes. What she had always expected to see. Shock. Pity. Disgust. Of course he would be disgusted. The shame had always been too much to handle and Kelly wasn't about to try and deal with it just now.

'Don't, Fletch.' Her words were a warning. 'Don't…say…anything.'

What could he have said? He had already said it all in three words.

You're safe now.

His need to protect Kelly had been all that had mattered. The shock that she had something so horrific that she needed to be protected from, and the hurt in her life that she'd never given him any hint of, had not surfaced properly until well after the event. Until hours after Kath's successful surgery and the unexpected end to the night's dramatic events.

Fletch had hung around the emergency department waiting until Kath came out of Theatre. He had seen Callum come in several times with new patients. A heart attack victim, a teenager with possible appendicitis and finally a service station attendant who had been assaulted during an armed hold-up.

'I was wondering if you'd still be here.' Callum loaded the stretcher back into the ambulance and then came to stand next to Fletch, who had gone outside for a breath of fresh air. 'Have you seen Kelly?'

'No.' Fletch rubbed a hand across his forehead wearily. 'She hasn't spoken to anyone except the police. She's up in the intensive care unit at the moment with her mother.'

'How did the surgery go?'

'Great. She's breathing on her own and regained consciousness enough to recognise Kelly. I think she'll be OK.'

'That's good news. How's Kelly?'

'I don't know.' Fletch sighed. 'She doesn't want to talk to me yet.'

Callum gave him a curious glance. 'You've known Kelly longer than I have. Did you know about her father?'

'No.' The monosyllable couldn't begin to convey the hurt. Why hadn't she told him something that important? They had been engaged. Kelly had said she loved him—that she still loved him. How could you love someone and not share a secret like that? As far as Fletch had known, Kelly's father had never been around. The only family he had ever met had been her mother.

'Seems that he's only just got out of prison.'

'What?' The new information was as much of a shock as the problem Kelly's father had with alcohol. 'How do you know that?'

'We spent quite a bit of time with the police before we were allowed onto the scene of the hold-up we just went to. I was talking to one of the guys who went out to Kelly's house. He knew rather a lot about Jack Drummond.'

'What was he in prison for?'

'Drunk driving.'

'How long was he in for?'

'He served five years of a seven-year sentence.'

So he'd been in prison well before he had even met Kelly. He hadn't been a part of her life. Or he had been a part of her life that both she and her mother had been trying to forget. Something was falling into place. Or trying to.

'Seven years is a pretty stiff sentence for drunk driving.'

'Not when you're driving when already disqualified for the same offence. Especially not when you lose control of the car and wipe out someone's grandmother on a zebra crossing.'

Fletch swore softly. 'That's appalling!'

Callum's smile was wry. 'Hardly surprising Kelly didn't want to advertise it, is it?'

'No.' And it was hardly surprising that she had an intolerant attitude to alcohol. Or to someone who became abusive when apparently drunk.

'Well, she won't need to worry about him any more.'

'I guess not. He'll go down for a long stretch after the assault on Kath.'

Callum's eyebrow rose. 'You haven't heard, then?'

'Heard what?'

His companion whistled softly. 'When Jack Drummond got away from Security here he ran into the park. A guard chased him but lost sight of him. They think he must have slipped over the bank and into the river. They found him a couple of hours ago.'

'And?' Fletch thought he knew the answer already but he wanted to hear it said.

'Dead,' Callum confirmed. 'The water was only knee deep but he'd got his foot caught in a tree root. Probably too drunk to figure out he only had to stay standing up.'

'Does Kelly know?'

'I would think so. That's why I was wondering how she was.'

'It's probably a relief.'

'He was still her father. No matter how ashamed of him she was. It's not going to be easy.'

'Kelly's a strong person.' Fletch had never known just how strong she was. His smile was poignant. 'It's just that sometimes she chooses the wrong things to be strong about.'

Like choosing to shoulder the burden of a traumatic past alone. Like choosing to give up the man she loved because the fear that he might turn out to be like her father was too much to face. Fletch could see everything so clearly now. He had always loved the courage and determination with which Kelly tackled life. The knowledge of what must have fostered those attributes made him love her even more. If only he'd known. If only he'd given her the chance. But he'd been too sick to do that two years ago and he had been too determined not to allow himself to admit how he felt since she'd come back into his life. He'd pushed her away only hours ago. Told her that he didn't want her physical touch. That he didn't want *her*.

It was understandable that she didn't want him anywhere near her at the moment, but Fletch had to try again. He went up to the intensive care unit only to find the chair beside Kath Drummond's bed was empty.

'We've persuaded Kelly to get a few hours' sleep,' the charge nurse told Fletch. 'She's on the couch in the relatives' room with a good dose of sedative on board. I wouldn't disturb her unless you have to.'

'I'll come back tomorrow,' Fletch said. 'I'd better get some sleep myself before I come on duty. How's Kath?'

'Doing as well as can be expected. She's holding her own at the moment and if she gets through the next twelve hours or so without deterioration we'll be able to be a lot more confident about a good prognosis.'

Fletch nodded. 'Tell Kelly I came in, would you?' He hesitated. 'Tell her I think I understand now.'

'I'll pass it on.' The nurse gave Fletch a curious glance. 'Was that all?'

Fletch nodded slowly but then paused. 'Tell her...that I'm sorry.'

Sorry for what? Kelly wondered. Sorry that her mother was seriously injured? That her father was dead? That her father had always been a loser? Or was he sorry that he didn't want her any more despite her confession that she still loved him? There was too much to be sorry for. And Kelly didn't want his pity. She didn't even want to see Fletch again just yet. She had more than enough to cope with.

It was a long, slow day. Her mother drifted in and out of semi-consciousness but was kept sedated enough to prevent her speaking. The bank of monitors around the bed indicated that Kath's condition was stable and by that afternoon a steady improvement became noticeable. Kelly left the unit for an hour or so to have a meal and a walk outside. She returned to find she had missed another visit from Dr Neil Fletcher but her reaction was one of relief rather than disappointment.

'He said to call him if you wanted,' the charge nurse relayed.

Wanted what? Kelly wondered. Company? Conversation? *Him?* The temptation to pick up the phone was easily dismissed.

The dose of sedative her mother was receiving was reduced that evening. Kelly sat by the bed, hoping that her mother might wake. She dozed fitfully in her chair off and on as the hours crept past.

'You're exhausted, darling.' The quiet words made Kelly's eyes fly open.

'Mum!' The joyous smile couldn't mask the concern. 'You're awake. How are you feeling?'

'My head hurts a bit,' Kath whispered. 'How long have I been in here?'

'Getting on for thirty hours. You had surgery last night and you've been asleep all of today and most of the night. It's 4 a.m. now.'

Kath's fingers squeezed Kelly's weakly. 'I still feel tired.'

'You need to rest,' Kelly told her. 'You're going to be fine.'

'I thought...I thought he was going to kill me this time.'

'I know.' Kelly touched the uninjured side of her mother's face gently. 'He'll never be able to hurt you again, Mum, I promise.' It wasn't the time to tell Kath about the final event of last night. The news could wait until she was stronger. Until Kelly herself felt strong enough to help her deal with it. 'You need to rest,' Kelly repeated. 'We'll look after you.'

'You need to rest, too. Go home, Kelly. I'll be fine.' Kath's eyes drifted shut again.

The medical staff backed up Kath's advice with increasing persuasion over the next few hours. 'We'll keep her on a low level of sedation for a while yet. She'll be asleep for the rest of tonight and probably most of the day tomorrow. Go home and rest, Kelly. We'll call you if there's any change.'

Kelly gave in. She knew she needed to rest and, even more, she needed some time alone. Time to try and sort through the jumble of emotions she was struggling to contain. There was just too much to think about. Too much to be sorry for.

The taxi driver had to wake her.

'We're here,' he explained. 'You've had a good nap, haven't you? That'll be forty-five dollars.'

'Really?' Kelly blinked. The sudden wakening into the strong sunshine and the rural surroundings made it difficult to focus.

'It's a long way from town,' the driver said defensively.

Kelly smiled. It had been the fact that she had slept so soundly on the journey home that had surprised her, not the amount of the taxi fare. The twenty-minute nap had been enough to take the edge off her exhaustion. Now all Kelly wanted was a quiet spot in the shade somewhere so she could sit and think quietly. Or, better yet, not think at all. She just wanted to be here. At home. Safe.

The call on her mobile phone was an intrusion but it couldn't be ignored in case it concerned her mother.

'Kelly speaking.'

She listened for a few seconds. 'Oh, no! I don't believe it.'

She listened for longer this time. 'No, I'm sorry. It's just not possible.'

The head shake was firm a few seconds later. 'No,' she repeated. 'I can't. I'm sorry.'

Kelly shook her head again, this time with disbelief. She stared at her phone. She couldn't cope with another call like that and it was highly likely there would be another one. But what about the hospital? If she turned her phone off they wouldn't be able to call her if they needed to. Kelly chewed her lip. She could call the intensive care unit herself to check on her mother's condition.

She would do it soon. Just as soon as she'd had a little more time to herself. Time without having to field an extraordinary demand on her like the one that had just been made.

Kelly pushed the button to switch her mobile phone off.

CHAPTER TEN

THE packing was less haphazard than it appeared.

Fletch tucked the knee pads into a side compartment of the pack. He rolled up the overalls and pushed them in on top of the clothing and toiletry articles he had pulled together. The heavy boots and helmet had taken up more room than expected but there was still enough space—just—to slot in the dust mask and protective goggles. A glance at his watch confirmed there was still plenty of time. Check-in at the airport was a little over an hour away. Time enough for a quick phone call.

'Joe? It's Fletch. Did Dave get hold of you?'

'I'm just packing. Can you believe it?'

'Hasn't really sunk in yet. There seems to be more than a suggestion that this is no accident.'

'Someone saw the package and raised the alarm so a lot of people got out before it went

275

off. I think we have a serial bomber who likes targeting shopping malls.'

'It doesn't make any sense. There's no motive. Christchurch was an unlikely enough place for a terrorist strike. But Dunedin?'

'I know.' Joe's tone acknowledged the smaller size and relative obscurity of the city five hours' drive south of Christchurch. 'Weird, isn't it? I'd better get going, Fletch. I can't find my helmet. I'll see you at the airport.'

'OK. Oh…Joe?'

'Yep?'

'Is Kelly coming?'

'No. Dave said she refused. I imagine it's because of her mother's condition.'

'Her mum's quite stable now. She's on the mend.'

'I know. And Dave's a bit worried. He's only managed to pull together a minimum team and it's going to take a lot longer to get anyone down from the north island.'

'It doesn't sound like it's nearly as big a collapse as the one at Westgate Mall. It might only be a day trip. Kath's not even expecting her to visit again before tonight.'

'Kelly apparently said it just wasn't possible.'

Fletch thought he knew the reason why. 'I'll ring her myself. Maybe I can persuade her.'

'Good idea. Have to go, Fletch. That's my doorbell. Wendy's coming here to catch a ride.'

'Hang on. Have you got Kelly's mobile number?'

The possibility that the Drummond property was outside the coverage area was unlikely. Kelly must have switched off her phone. Fletch took another glance at his watch. It would take twenty minutes to get to the daffodil farm but it was only fifteen minutes from there to the airport. The check-in time might not be that tight. He punched another number into his phone, spoke briefly and then moved swiftly. The pack was dumped on the back seat of his car and Fletch backed rapidly from his driveway, turned left and headed south through the city. There was just enough time.

He had to see Kelly.

*　　*　　*

The house appeared deserted. Fletch gave up knocking on the front door and walked around the cottage. Kelly's car was there. The ICU staff had told him that Kelly had ordered a taxi and that she was planning to go home and sleep, but there were no curtains drawn to block out the bright sunshine and the back door was wide open.

'Kelly? Are you there?'

She had to be here somewhere. The thought that he might have to leave without talking to Kelly, without touching her, was suddenly unbearable. Kelly had to know that he understood now. That he realised why things had gone so terribly wrong between them and that it was possible to start again. It had to be possible if Kelly had meant what she'd said to him.

The property wasn't huge. Five acres or so at most. Fletch stood on the back verandah and shaded his eyes against the glare of the sun. It gave him an odd feeling to be seeing the place again. He had almost forgotten that he and Kelly had even toyed with the attractive possibility of building their own house on the property at some stage in the future. They had decided they would position it on the other side of the daffodil fields, near where the small stream bordered the property. That dream seemed so long ago and yet it all looked just the same. The large vegetable garden, the hen-house, the small orchard and then the daffodils. A huge, joyful mass of colour in all shades of yellow, orange and white. The kind of colours it would be impossible not to be uplifted by. In the centre of the vibrant display was a splash of dark, restful green. The branches of the ancient weeping elm formed an umbrella that created a shady oasis. Fletch smiled. If he needed a place to restore peace to his soul then that would be exactly where he would choose to sit.

It was exactly where Kelly had chosen to sit. She could see Fletch approaching through the rows of flowers. The scene had an inevitability about it that precluded any movement to disturb the waiting. No smile of greeting touched her lips and Kelly's focused gaze was the only acknowledgement of Fletch's presence as he halted and then dropped to a crouch in front of her.

'Hi.' Fletch wasn't smiling either. He looked more serious than Kelly had ever seen him look. 'I came to find you, Kelly,' he said unnecessarily. 'I thought you might like a ride to the airport.'

'I'm not going.'

'But we need you.'

'No.' Kelly shook her head sadly. 'No, you don't. You'll manage just fine without me, Fletch.'

It was only a matter of inches from Fletch's hand to where Kelly's lay, locked in front of her knees which she had drawn up to her chest, as she sat leaning back against the trunk of the old tree. He had to make an effort to restrain himself from touching her. She was too caught up in her own grief right now. Too controlled. And Fletch couldn't afford to shatter the secure space she had enclosed herself in.

'Your mum's doing so well. I went to see her just before I left the hospital. She was sitting up and having a cup of tea.'

Kelly nodded. 'She's going to be fine— thanks to you. She might well have died if you hadn't been there.'

'We wouldn't have found her if I hadn't needed to take you home.'

Kelly's lips twitched into a reluctant smile. 'And you wouldn't have taken me home if I hadn't had too much to drink. Ironic, isn't it?'

Fletch held her gaze. 'I'm sorry about your father, Kelly. I had no idea.'

'Of course you didn't.' Kelly's glance slid sideways. 'How could you? I made very sure that nobody knew about him. It was much easier once he was locked away. I persuaded Mum to start a new life for herself and we found this place. I helped her to buy it. By the time I met you, things were going so well it was even easy for me to forget the past. I *wanted* to forget.' Her eyes met Fletch's only briefly. 'And don't be sorry he's dead because *I'm* not.'

But Fletch could see the grief. Maybe it wasn't grief for Jack Drummond but grief for the father she'd never really had. A man she had once loved who had let her down too often and too badly to ever forgive.

'I wish you had told me, Kelly,' he said sadly. 'I would have understood.'

'No.' Kelly shook her head. 'You would have met him when he was sober and you would have found him as charming as everyone else did. Even Mum never understood completely. She loved him. She thought alcoholism was a disease—that he couldn't really help it, and that one day they would get through it. And they would only get through it if she stuck it out and stayed with him.' Kelly was unaware of the tears that rolled down her cheeks. 'Even the first time I called the police when he had hurt Mum she refused to press charges. I was fourteen and I'd never hated anyone as much as I hated Dad.'

Kelly scrubbed at her cheeks as the tears became too numerous to stay unnoticed. 'He swore he'd never touch alcohol again after that but I knew he would. I just waited for it—like I had for as long as I could remember. Waited to smell it on his breath when he was late home. Waited for the fight he'd have to pick with Mum, no matter how hard she tried to avoid it. And there was never anything I could do to stop it.'

Fletch simply listened, hearing the pain of a child's life spent in fear of a monster that couldn't be controlled. A life of trying to avoid the inevitable and of trying to protect someone who should have been protecting her. He felt a flash of anger against Kath, who had allowed her only child to suffer that fear.

Kelly seemed to read the direction of his thoughts. 'It wasn't Mum's fault. She really believed she was doing the right thing and there were long periods when everything seemed fine.'

Fine. Apart from the waiting. Apart from building the knowledge of how destructive an addiction could be.

'After the…the accident, even Mum had to give up on him. She had no intention of letting him come home when he got out of prison. She loved this place from the moment we found it. It's never made quite enough to pay the mortgage but we've managed between us. Mum's put her heart and soul into making it a home for herself. And for me if I still wanted it. I thought it was safe for me to go away for a while. To try and sort my own life out.'

To get away from him. From the possibility that she'd been about to step into the same kind of nightmare her mother had lived with. That she had grown up with.

Kelly's voice hardened a touch. 'But then he started to write to her a year or so ago. To tell her how well his rehabilitation programme had gone. And she started writing back. When I found out that he had parole coming up I knew I had to come home. To persuade Mum that the risk just wasn't worth it.'

That she could never trust him. That she deserved to be selfish for once in her life. Echoes of that overheard conversation made sense now. Perfect sense.

'I'm not an alcoholic, Kelly.'

'I know that now. And I know I treated you badly by walking out but...' Kelly's voice caught. 'But I knew that if I saw you again— if I spoke to you and you promised it would never happen again—then there was no way I could leave. I loved you so much I would have stayed even if you *had* been an alcoholic. I would have let you convince me...until the next time. And there I'd be, waiting again. The only way I could guarantee that wasn't going to happen was to get as far away as possible.'

'I loved you that much as well.' Fletch reached out now. His hands covered Kelly's. 'I was so sick I was sure I was going to die. I needed you so badly then, Kelly. When I found you had gone there seemed no point in living at all.'

Kelly's hands opened. She caught Fletch's fingers with her own. 'I'll never forgive myself for that. Never.'

'Yes, you will.' Fletch smiled slowly. 'Because I forgive you. And it's over now. I didn't die and I'm not going to. I'm fine. You didn't know and you can't take any blame for that.'

'And you didn't know about my father.'

'And neither of us knew that we'd end up on that USAR course together.' Fletch squeezed the hands now locked with his own. 'I couldn't believe I was seeing you again. I wouldn't let myself believe I could still feel the same way about you. I had been so hurt and so angry it was easy enough to convince myself that I didn't want to go there again.' He disengaged one hand and touched Kelly's cheek, brushing away a half-dried tear. 'But I knew. Even before I knew about your father and could understand why you acted the way you did. I knew the moment you kissed me that nothing could ever really change how I feel about you.'

His hand was cupping her face now with a gentle strength that Kelly could feel flowing through her entire body.

'I love you, Kelly. Knowing what I know now has only made me love you more. I love your courage, your strength—your loyalty to the people you love.'

Kelly swallowed to try and ease the constriction in her throat. 'I love you, Fletch,' she whispered. 'I never stopped loving you.'

'I hope you never will.' Fletch bent towards Kelly and touched her lips with his. A gentle kiss that spoke of commitment rather than passion. 'Because I'm never, ever going to stop loving you.'

The smile they shared was as simple as that kiss. Nothing more was needed for the moment. They both knew that when the time was right they could revisit the kind of intimacy that only a love this deep could produce. That time was not yet here.

'How quickly could you pack your rescue gear if you had to?'

'It's been packed ever since I cleaned it up after our first call-out.' Her smile was a little embarrassed. 'Just like Kyle.'

Fletch stood up. 'The plane for Dunedin is due to take off in ten minutes. I called Dave to tell him I was coming here on the way and he's holding the plane until I get there.' Fletch's smile was an invitation. 'Or until *we* get there.'

'I said I couldn't go.' Kelly gazed up at Fletch.

'But we need you, Kelly.' Fletch held out his hand and then smiled again. '*I* need you.'

Kelly didn't hesitate. There was no need because the choice had already been made. Maybe it had been made a long time ago and Kelly had only just realised its significance. She reached up and linked her hand with that of Fletch. They would face this crisis in just the same way they would face anything else that the rest of their lives had to offer.

Together.

MEDICAL ROMANCE™

Large Print

Titles for the next three months…

July

OUTBACK MARRIAGE	Meredith Webber
THE BUSH DOCTOR'S CHALLENGE	Carol Marinelli
THE PREGNANT SURGEON	Jennifer Taylor
THE GP'S SECRET	Abigail Gordon

August

OUTBACK ENCOUNTER	Meredith Webber
THE NURSE'S RESCUE	Alison Roberts
A VERY SINGLE MIDWIFE	Fiona McArthur
A SURGEON FOR KATE	Janet Ferguson

September

DOCTORS IN FLIGHT	Meredith Webber
SAVING DR TREMAINE	Jessica Matthews
THE SPANISH CONSULTANT	Sarah Morgan
THE GREEK DOCTOR'S BRIDE	Margaret Barker

MILLS & BOON®

Live the emotion

0604 LP 1P Medical